D1135346

# THIRTEEN O'CLOCK
## AND
## OTHER STORIES

# Thirteen O'Clock

## and
## Other Stories

by
ENID BLYTON

*Illustrations by*
*DOROTHY HAMILTON*

AWARD PUBLICATIONS

ISBN 0 86163 143 9

Text copyright 1947 Darrell Waters Limited
Illustrations copyright © 1985 Award Publications Limited

First published 1945 as *Enid Blyton's Sunny Storybook*
by Hodder & Stoughton Limited

This edition entitled *Thirteen O'Clock and Other Stories*
First published 1985
Third impression 1988

Published by Award Publications Limited,
Spring House, Spring Place, London NW5 3BH

Printed in Great Britain

# CONTENTS

# 1

## *Jinky the Jumping Frog*

Jinky was a little green jumping frog who lived in the toy cupboard with all the other toys. He had a spring inside him that made him able to jump high up in the air, and he often frightened the toys by his enormous jumps. He didn't *mean* to frighten them, but, you see, he couldn't walk or run, so his only way of getting about was to jump.

'I'm sorry if I startle you,' he said to the angry toys. 'Please try and get used to my big hops. I can't do anything else you see.'

The toys thought he was silly. He was a shy little frog, and he didn't say much, so the toys thought he was stupid. They left him out of all their games at night, and he was often very lonely when he sat in a corner of the toy cupboard and watched the toys playing with one of the nursery balls.

Now the prettiest and daintiest of all the toys was Silvertoes, the fairy doll. She was perfectly lovely, and she had a silver crown on her head, a frock of finest gauze that stood out all round her, a pair of shining silver wings, and a little silver wand which she always carried in her right hand. Everyone loved her, and the green frog loved her the most of all.

But she wouldn't even look at him! He had once made her jump by hopping suddenly down by her, and she had never forgiven him. So Jinky watched her from a distance and wished and wished she would smile at him just once. But she never did.

One night there was a bright moon outside, and the brownie who lived inside the apple tree just by the nursery window, came and called on the toys.

'Let's all go out into the garden and dance in the moonlight,' he said. 'It's lovely and warm, and we could have a fine time together.'

Out went all the toys through the window! They climbed down the apple tree, and slid to the grass below. Then they began to dance in the moonlight. They all took partners except the green frog, who was left out. He sat patiently on the grass, watching the other toys, and wishing that he could dance too.

There was such a noise of talking and laughing that no one noticed a strange throbbing sound up in the sky. No one, that is, except the green frog. He heard it and he looked up. He saw a bright silver aeroplane, about as big as a rook, circling round and round above the lawn.

Then someone looked down from the aeroplane and Jinky shivered with fright – for who should it be but Sly-One, the gnome who lived in Bracken Country, far away. He was a sly and unpleasant person, and nobody, fairy or toy, liked to have anything to do with him.

'I wonder what he wants to come here for tonight!' said Jinky to himself. 'He's up to some mischief, I'm sure!'

He was! He suddenly swooped down in his aeroplane, landed near the toys, ran up to the fairy doll, snatched her away from the teddy bear who was dancing with her, and ran off with her to his aeroplane!

How she screamed! 'Help! Help! Oh, please save me, toys!'

The toys were so astonished that they stood and gaped at the bold gnome. He threw the fairy doll into his aeroplane, jumped in himself, and away he went into the air! Then the toys suddenly saw what was happening, and began to shout.

'You wicked gnome! Bring her back at once! We'll put you in prison if you don't!'

The gnome felt quite safe in the air. He circled round and round the toys and bent over the side of his aeroplane to laugh at them.

'Ha, ha!' he said. 'Put me in prison did you say? Well, come and catch me!'

To the great anger of the toys he flew very low indeed, just above their heads. The teddy bear, who was tall, tried to jump up and hang on to the aeroplane, but he couldn't quite reach it. He was in despair.

'Whatever shall we do?' he cried to the toys. 'We can't possibly rescue the fairy doll in that horrid aeroplane.'

'Ha, ha!' laughed the gnome again, swooping down to the toys – and just at that moment the green frog saw his chance! He would do a most ENORMOUS jump and see if he could leap right on to the aeroplane.

He jumped. My goodness me, what a leap that was! You should have seen him! He jumped right up into the air, and reached out his front feet for the aeroplane. And he just managed it! He hung on to the tail of the 'plane, and then managed to scramble up. The gnome had not seen him.

The toys were too astonished to say a word. They stood with open mouths looking up at the brave green frog, and

he signed to them to say nothing about him. He thought that if the gnome did not know he was there he might be able to rescue the fairy doll without much difficulty.

The gnome flew off in his aeroplane. He wanted to reach Bracken Cottage that night, and he meant to marry the fairy doll in the morning. He thought it would be lovely to have such a pretty creature cooking his dinner and mending his clothes.

The frog crouched down on the tail of the aeroplane. It was very cold there, but he didn't mind. He was simply delighted to think that he would have a chance to do something for the pretty fairy doll.

At last Sly-One arrived at Bracken Cottage. He glided down and landed in the big field at the back of his house. Out he jumped, and turned to the fairy doll, who was cold, frightened and miserable.

'Wait here a minute and I'll just go and unlock the door,' he said. 'Then I'll

come back and fetch you.' He ran off –
and as soon as he had gone the green
frog hopped down into the seat beside
the fairy doll.

She nearly screamed with fright, but
he stopped her.

'Sh!' he said. 'It's only me, Jinky the
jumping frog. I've come to save you. Do
you think we can fly back in this
aeroplane?'

'Oh, Jinky, I'm so glad to see you,'
sobbed the poor doll. 'Look, you jerk
that handle up, and the aeroplane
should fly up into the air.'

Jinky jerked the handle in front of
him, but nothing happened. The gnome
had stopped the engine, and of course,
it wouldn't move. Jinky was in despair.
He didn't in the least know how to fly
the 'plane, and he was terribly afraid
that if it did begin to fly there would be
an accident.

'It's no good,' he said, hopping out of
the seat. 'I can't make it go. Come on,
fairy doll, get out, and jump on my
back. I'll leap off with you, and perhaps

we can escape that way.'

'Take the handle out of the aeroplane,'
said the doll. 'Then that nasty gnome
can't fly after us in it. He won't be able
to make it go up!'

'Good idea!' said the frog, and he tore
off the handle. He put it into his mouth
for he was afraid to throw it anywhere
in case the gnome found it again. He
thought he would carry it a little way
and then throw it into a bush. The fairy

16

doll climbed on to his back, and held tight.

'Now please, don't be frightened,' said the jumping frog. 'I shall jump high, but you will be quite safe. I can't walk or run, you know.'

'*I* shan't be frightened,' said the fairy doll, clinging to his back. 'I think you are the dearest, bravest, handsomest, strongest frog that ever I saw!'

Well! How Jinky swelled with pride when he heard that! He looked behind him to see that the gnome was still far away - but, oh my goodness, he was running back from his cottage at top speed, for he had seen the doll get out of the aeroplane!

Jinky wasted no more time but leapt high into the air and down again. Again and again he jumped, and each jump took him further away from the gnome, who had gone to his aeroplane to fly after them.

When he found that the starting handle had gone, he was very angry. He jumped out of the 'plane and ran to his garage. He opened the doors, and in a few moments Jinky heard the sound of a car engine roaring.

'Oh, my!' he thought in dismay. 'If he comes after me in a car I shan't have any chance at all!'

On he went, leaping as far as he could each time. The fairy doll clung to him, and called to him to go faster still. Behind them came the gnome's car, driven at a fearful speed.

Then crash! There came a tremendous noise, and Jinky turned round to see what had happened. The gnome had driven so fast round a corner that he had gone smash into a tree, and his car was broken to pieces. Sly-One jumped out unhurt, very angry indeed. He shook his fist at the jumping frog, and looked at his broken car. Then he ran to a cottage nearby and thumped at the door.

A sleepy goblin came, and asked him what he wanted.

'Lend me your bicycle now!' demanded the gnome. 'I want it to chase a wicked frog.'

The goblin brought it out and the gnome jumped into the saddle. Off he pedalled at a furious rate after the frog and the doll.

'He's got a bicycle now!' shouted the fairy doll to Jinky. 'Oh, hurry up, hurry up!'

Jinky jumped as fast as he could, but the doll was heavy and he began to be afraid that he would never escape. Behind him came the gnome on the bicycle, ringing his bell loudly all the time.

Suddenly the frog came to a village, and in the middle of the street stood a policeman with red wings. He held out his hand to stop Jinky and the doll, but with a tremendous jump the frog leapt right over him and was at the other end of the village before the angry policeman knew what had happened. Then he heard the loud ringing of Sly-One's bicycle bell, and turned to stop the gnome. He held out his hand sternly.

But the gnome couldn't and wouldn't stop! He ran right into the astonished policeman, and knocked him flat on his face. Bump! The gnome flew off his bicycle and landed right in the middle of the duck-pond near by. The bicycle ran off by itself and smashed against a wall.

How angry the policeman was! He jumped to his feet and marched over to the gnome. 'I arrest you for not stopping when I told you to, and for knocking me down,' he said.

But the gnome slipped away from him, and ran down the street after the doll and the frog. The policeman ran after him, and off went the two, helter-skelter down the road.

The frog had quite a good start by

now, and he was leaping for all he was worth. The doll was telling him all that had happened, and when he heard how the gnome had run into the policeman, he laughed so much that he got a stitch in his side and had to stop to rest.

'Oh, don't laugh!' begged the doll. 'It really isn't funny. Do get on, Jinky.'

His stitch was soon better, and on he went again, while some way behind him panted the gnome and the policeman. The frog felt sure he could jump faster than the gnome could run, so he wasn't so worried as he had been. For two more hours he jumped and jumped, and at last he came to the place where the toys had been dancing last night. They had all gone back to the nursery, very sad because they felt sure that the fairy doll and the frog were lost forever.

The frog jumped in at the window, and the fairy doll slid off his back. How the toys shouted and clapped their hands in glee! How they praised the brave frog, and begged his pardon for the unkind things they had said and done to him. And you should have seen his face when the fairy doll suddenly threw her arms around his neck and kissed him! He was so pleased that he jumped all round the room for joy.

Suddenly there was a shout outside. It was the gnome still running, and the policeman after him! The gnome was so angry that he meant to run into the nursery and fight the jumping frog!

Then the teddy bear did a clever

22

thing. He put an empty box just underneath the window, and waited by it with the lid in his hands. The gnome jumped through the window straight into the box, and the bear clapped the lid down on him!

When the policeman came into the room too, the bear bowed gravely to him and handed him the box neatly tied round with string.

'Here is your prisoner,' he said. 'Please take him away, he is making such a noise.'

The surprised policeman thanked the bear, bowed to the toys, and went out of the window again. Then the toys sat down and had a good laugh, but the one who laughed the loudest of all was Jinky, the little green frog!

23

# 2

## *The Kickaway Shoes*

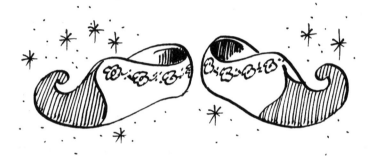

Skip and Jump were very busy brownies.

They had been spring-cleaning their cottage from top to bottom – and my, what a lot of rubbish they had turned out!

'Look at that!' said Skip, pointing to an enormous pile of old kettles, old books, and old boots and shoes he had put in their back garden. 'Whatever are we going to do with all this rubbish?'

'And look at my pile of rubbish too!' said Jump. Skip looked. It certainly was an even bigger pile than his. There was a broken-down iron bedstead, two chipped vases, an old enamel candlestick, four saucepans with holes in – oh, and heaps more things.

'What are we going to do with them?' asked Skip.

'We can't burn them; they won't burn.'

25

'And we haven't a dustman in our village,' said Jump. 'So we can't ask him to collect our rubbish.'

'And we are *not* going to throw these old things into the ditches as lots of untidy people do,' said Skip. 'That would spoil the countryside. So what *are* we going to do?'

'I say – what about borrowing those Kickaway Shoes belonging to Grumpy Gnome!' cried Jump, all at once. 'They would soon take all our rubbish away!'

'Ooh, yes,' said Skip. 'But I'm afraid of the Grumpy Gnome. He's so bad-tempered, and I don't trust him.'

'Well, if we pay him for the loan of his magic shoes, he can't be angry with us,' said Jump. 'Just think, Skip! Whatever we kick with the Kickaway Shoes immediately disappears! Its wonderful! If I kicked that old saucepan there with a Kickaway Shoe, it would fly away and we'd never see it again! Ooh, it wouldn't take us long to get rid of all our rubbish then, would it?'

'And what fun it would be to do some

magic kicking!' cried Skip, jumping about in excitement. 'What fun! Let's go and ask Grumpy Gnome now.'

'We'll take a piece of gold with us,' said Jump, running to his purse, which was on the mantelpiece. 'He is sure to charge us a lot. He is a greedy, selfish horrid fellow, and nobody likes him. We won't stay long, in case he puts a nasty spell on us.'

Off went the two brownies in great excitement. Jump had the piece of gold

safely in his pocket. They soon came to Grumpy's cottage. It was built into the hillside, and there was a red door with a big black knocker. Jump knocked loudly. Rat-tat-tat!

The Grumpy Gnome opened the door and glared at them. He was a nasty-looking person. He had yellow whiskers and a very long nose. His eyes were small and he wore on his head a round red cap with little silver bells all round the rim. They rang when he walked. It was a magic cap, and he never took it off, not even to brush his hair. So nobody knew whether he had any hair or not.

'What do you want?' he said, in his loud deep voice.

'Please would you lend us your Kickaway Shoes?' asked Jump politely. 'We will pay you for the loan of them.'

'I shall want a piece of gold,' said the Grumpy Gnome, nodding his head till all the silver bells on his cap rang loudly.

'We have brought you a piece,' said

Jump, and he showed the gold to Grumpy. The gnome's little eyes shone at the sight of the gold, and he suddenly grabbed it and put it into his own pocket.

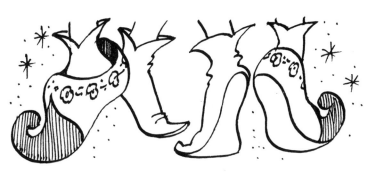

'Here are the shoes,' he said, taking down a curious pair of shoes from a shelf behind the door. They were bright yellow, and had turned-up ends of red-painted iron to kick with. The two brownies took them eagerly. They thanked the gnome and turned to go.

'Bring them back tonight without fail,' commanded Grumpy. He shook his head fiercely at them, making all the silver bells tinkle again, and then slammed the door.

'What an unpleasant creature he is, to be sure,' said Skip, looking quite pale. 'I was really afraid he was going to turn us into black-beetles or something! You know, he is supposed to do that to people he doesn't like. And once he turned a cheeky pixie into a currant bun and ate him! Oooh my, he's a horrid person!'

The brownies hurried home with the magic shoes. When they got there they each put a shoe on their right foot and danced about in glee.

'We've got the Kickaway Shoes, we've got the Kickaway Shoes!' they cried. They made such a noise that Whiskers, their big black cat, came out to see what they were doing.

'Hello, Whiskers, darling!' cried the brownies, who were both very fond of their cat. 'Look at our magic shoes.'

Whiskers sniffed at them and then hurriedly backed away. She had smelt the magic in them and was afraid. She went off to a corner of the garden.

'Now let's start kicking away all our

rubbish!' cried Skip. 'Come on! Watch me kick away this old saucepan!'

He stood behind the saucepan, lifted his right foot and gave the saucepan an enormous kick with the iron end of the Kickaway Shoe! Bang!

The saucepan shot into the air and flew away! My, how it flew! The brownies watched it going through the air until it was just a black speck. Then they couldn't see it any longer.

'I wonder where it's gone to,' said Jump.

'It's gone to the Land of Rubbish,' said Skip. 'Now it's your turn, Jump. Kick that vase away!'

Jump kicked with all his might. The vase broke into a hundred pieces, and each piece flew through the air at top speed. They soon disappeared. The brownies giggled. This was great fun!

'We'll both kick away this nasty old bedstead,' said Skip. 'It's so big it wants two people to kick it, I'm sure!'

They both kicked with all their might. At once the bedstead rose into the air, and to the great delight of the brownies, and to the enormous surprise of the pixies down in the village, the old iron bedstead flew off through the air, looking smaller and smaller the further it flew. It was most exciting.

The brownies laughed till the tears came into their eyes. They were having a glorious time. They kicked away the candlesticks, the old boots and the tin kettles. They kicked away a pile of books and a broken spade. They kicked dozens of things and shouted in glee when they saw them all flying off in the air, never to come back.

At last there was nothing but an old basket left. Skip gave it a hard kick, and it rose into the air - but oh, goodness, what a dreadful thing! Whiskers, the cat, had curled herself up in that basket and Skip didn't know she was there! When the basket rose up in the air Whiskers shot out and she and the basket flew along together at top speed!

Whiskers mewed loudly, but it was

# The Kickaway Shoes

no use. She had to go to the Land of Rubbish, and soon the horrified brownies could see nothing of her but a tiny black speck far away in the sky.

'Oh! Oh!' cried Skip, the tears running down his cheeks in two streams. 'I didn't know Whiskers was in the basket! She'll never come back! Oh, my dear, darling old cat! Oh, Jump, she's gone!'

Jump sobbed, too. Both brownies loved their cat with all their hearts, and it was dreadful to think poor old Whiskers had been kicked off to the Land of Rubbish. How upset she would be! How lonely and frightened!

'Who will g-g-g-give her her m-m-m-m-milk?' wept Skip.

'Who will t-t-t-t-tuck her up in a warm rug at night?' sobbed Jump.

It was dreadful. The brownies couldn't think what to do! They put their arms round one another and cried so much that they made a puddle round their feet.

At last Skip had an idea.

'Let's go to Grumpy Gnome and ask him to tell us how to get Whiskers back!' he said. 'There is sure to be a spell to get her back.'

'Yes, yes!' cried Jump, wiping his eyes with his big yellow handkerchief. So off they set once more to Grumpy's cottage.

The gnome frowned at them when he opened the door.

'I said bring back the shoes tonight, not this afternoon,' he said crossly. 'I was just having a nap and you've wakened me.'

'Oh, please, Grumpy, we've come about something terribly important,' said Skip. 'We've kicked Whiskers, our lovely black cat, away by mistake, and we want you to tell us how to get her back!'

Grumpy's little eyes gleamed. 'Ha!' he thought. 'I can make some money out of this.'

'Well,' he said, aloud, 'That's certainly very serious. You will have to pay me a very large sum of money to

35

get her back. It's very hard to get a black cat back from the Land of Rubbish.'

'Oh dear,' said Jump and Skip. 'How much money do you want?'

'I want fifty pieces of gold!' said Grumpy.

'Ooooooo!' squealed Skip and Jump in horror. 'We only have three pieces! Get us our cat back for three pieces, Grumpy.'

'Certainly not,' said the gnome, pretending that he was shutting the door. 'Fifty pieces, or no cat!'

'Wait, wait!' said Jump. 'We've only three pieces, I tell you. What else will you take besides our three pieces of gold?'

'Well, I'll take your grandfather clock,' said Grumpy.

'Oh!' groaned the brownies sorrowfully. 'We do so love our old clock. But you shall have it.'

'And your rocking-chair,' said Grumpy, 'and the pair of lovely brass candlesticks you have on your mantelpiece.'

The brownies groaned again. They were proud of their rocking-chair and candlesticks. But still, they loved Whiskers more than all these things, so they sadly promised to go back home and fetch the gold, the clock, the chair and the candlesticks at once.

They ran off, crying. What a dreadful thing to have to give up all their nicest things to the horrid, greedy gnome! If he had been at all kind-hearted he would have been sorry about Whiskers, and would have got her back for nothing. But oh, the Grumpy Gnome had a heart as hard as stone!

Skip and Jump fetched out their big clock, their old rocking-chair, and the two candlesticks. Skip had the gold in his pocket. He carried the rocking-chair, too. Jump managed to take the grandfather clock and the candlesticks. They went slowly along, panting and puffing under their heavy loads.

Just as they got near Grumpy's cottage they met Bron, the head brownie of the village. He was most astonished to see Skip and Jump carrying such heavy things.

'Are you moving?' he asked.

'No,' said Skip. 'We are taking these to Grumpy.' Then he told Bron all that had happened, and how Grumpy had made them promise to give him their nicest things in return for getting back Whiskers from the Land of Rubbish.

'So that's why we are taking him our three gold pieces, our beautiful grandfather clock, our rocking-chair and our lovely candlesticks,' said Skip sadly. 'But you see, we must get Whiskers back. She'll be so lonely and so frightened.'

Bron frowned and looked as black as thunder when he heard about the greed and selfishness of the unkind gnome.

'Where are the Kickaway Shoes?' he asked.

'I've still got one on, and so has Skip,' said Jump, and he lifted up his right foot to show Bron.

'Give them to me,' said Bron.

In great surprise Skip and Jump took off the Kickaway Shoes and watched Bron put them on, one on each foot. Then they looked on in even greater surprise when he marched straight up to Grumpy's front door and banged hard on the knocker.

'RAT-A-TAT-TAT!'

The door flew open and out came Grumpy, looking very angry indeed.

'How dare you knock so loudly!' he began in a rage – then he stopped when

he saw it was Bron knocking and not Skip and Jump.

'I've just come to tell you something Grumpy Gnome,' said Bron, in a very fierce voice. 'I've come to tell you that you are the nastiest, greediest, unkindest gnome in the whole of the kingdom, and you don't deserve to live in this nice little village.'

'Oh, don't I?' said Grumpy, his little eyes glittering wickedly. 'Well, where do I deserve to live then? Tell me that!' And he turned to go indoors again.

'The best place for you is the Land of Rubbish!' shouted Bron, and before Grumpy could get inside his door, he kicked him hard with the iron points of the Kickaway Shoes – first with one shoe and then with the other.

Oh my goodness me! Grumpy gave a loud yell and rose up into the air, and then, still yelling, he flew on and on to the Land of Rubbish. The brownies watched him - and then suddenly Skip gave a cry.

'Oh, Bron! You've kicked him away before he told us how to get back dear old Whiskers. Oh dear, oh dear!'

'Don't worry!' said Bron cheerfully.

41

'A cat can always find its way home again, no matter where it's taken to. Whiskers will come back alright – and that wicked gnome knew it perfectly well. He was just robbing you of all these things for nothing. Take them back home again, put down a saucer of milk, and wait for Whiskers to come back.'

'Oh, thank you, Bron,' said the grateful little brownies. 'But what are you going to do with the Kickaway Shoes?'

'I shall keep them in my house, and then if anyone wants to borrow them he can do so for nothing,' said Bron. He put on his own shoes, and then, taking the Kickaway Shoes under his arm, he went off home, whistling loudly. He stopped every now and then to laugh when he thought of the Grumpy Gnome sailing through the air to the Land of Rubbish!

Skip and Jump staggered home again with all their belongings. They put them back in their places, and then they went to the larder for some milk. They poured out a saucerful, and put it down on the floor, ready for Whiskers when she came back.

Then they put the kettle on for tea, and toasted some muffins, for they really felt very hungry.

And would you believe it, just as they were sitting down to eat their tea, there came a mewing at the door! Skip leapt up and opened it – and there outside was dear old Whiskers, very tired and very hungry, for she had walked a very long way indeed.

'Darling old Whiskers!' cried the

brownies in delight, hugging her and
stroking her soft fur. 'Oh, we are glad
to see you! Here's some milk for you!
And shall we open a tin of sardines for
you, just for a treat?'

They were all so happy that evening.
Whiskers sat on Skip's knee first, and
then on Jump's, so that they might
share her properly between them. She
was just as glad to be back again as
they were to have her.

As for Grumpy Gnome, he's still in
the Land of Rubbish. And a very good
place for him, too!

# 3

## Thirteen O'clock

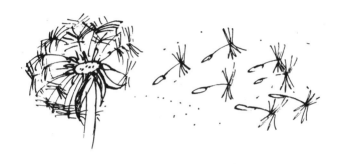

Once upon a time Sandy was walking home from school when he saw an extra fine dandelion clock.

'What a beauty!' he said, picking it with its stalk. 'I wonder if it will tell me the right time.'

He blew it – puff! A cloud of fluffy white seeds flew away. There were plenty left on the clock. He blew again – puff! More fluff flew away on the breeze. Puff! Puff! Puff! He counted as he blew.

'One o'clock! Two o'clock! Three! Four! Five! Six o'clock! Seven! Eight! Nine! Ten! Eleven o'clock! Twelve o'clock! *Thirteen o'clock*!'

At the thirteenth puff there was no fluff left on the dandelion clock at all. It was just an empty stalk.

And then things began to happen.

A noise of little voices was heard, and Sandy looked down at his feet. Round him was a crowd of pixies, shouting loudly.

'Did you say thirteen o'clock? Hi, did you say thirteen o'clock?'

'Yes,' said Sandy, in astonishment. 'The dandelion clock said thirteen o'clock.'

'Oh my goodness me, thirteen o'clock only happens once in a blue moon!' cried the biggest pixie. 'Whatever shall we do?'

'Why what's the matter?' asked Sandy. 'What are you so upset about?'

'Don't you know?' shouted all the

pixies together. 'Why, at thirteen o'clock
all the witches from Witchland fly on
broomsticks, and if they see any elf,
pixie, brownie or gnome out of Fairyland they catch them and take them
away. Oh dear, goodness gracious,
whatever shall we do?'

Sandy felt quite alarmed.

'Do they take little boys, too?' he
asked.

'We don't know, but they might,'
answered the biggest pixie. 'Hark! can
you hear the Witches' Wind blowing?'

Sandy listened. Yes, a wind was
blowing up, and it sounded a funny
sort of wind, all whispery and strange.

'That's the wind the witches use to
blow their broomsticks along,' said the
pixies. 'Little boy, you'd better run
home quickly.'

But Sandy wasn't going to leave the
little pixies alone. They were frightened,
so he felt he really must stay and look
after them.

'I'll stay with you,' he said. 'But do
you think you could make me as small

as you, because if I'm as big as this the witches will see me easily and catch me.'

'That's easy to do,' said the biggest pixie. 'Shut your eyes, put your hands over your ears and whisper "Hoona-looki-allo-pie" three times to yourself. Then you'll be as small as we are. When you want to get big again do exactly the same, but say the magic words backwards.'

Sandy felt excited. He shut his eyes and covered his ears with his hands. Then he whispered the magic words three times – and lo and behold, when he opened his eyes again he was as small as the pixies! They crowded round him, laughing and talking.

'I'm Gobbo,' said the biggest one, 'and this is my friend, Twinkle.'

Sandy solemnly shook hands with Gobbo and Twinkle. Then, as the wind grew louder, the pixies crowded together in alarm, and looked up at the sky.

'Where shall we go to hide?' said Twinkle. 'Oh, quick, think of somewhere, somebody, or the witches will be along and will take us prisoners!'

Everybody thought hard, and then Sandy had a good idea.

'As I ·came along I noticed an old saucepan thrown away in the hedge,' he said. 'Let's go and find it and get under it. It will hide us all beautifully.'

Off went all the pixies, following Sandy. He soon found the saucepan, and by pushing hard they managed to turn it upside-down over them, so that it quite hid them. There was a hole in the side out of which they could peep.

'I've dropped my handkerchief,' suddenly cried Twinkle, pointing to where a little red hanky lay on the ground some way off. 'I must go and get it.'

'No, don't,' said Gobbo. 'You'll be caught. The witches will be along any minute now. Hark how the wind is blowing!'

'But I must get it!' cried Twinkle. 'If I don't the witches will catch sight of it out there, and down they'll all come to see what it is. Then they'll sniff pixies nearby and come hunting under this saucepan for us.'

'Ooooooooh!' groaned all the pixies, in fright.

'Well, go and get it quickly!' said Gobbo to Twinkle. 'Hurry up!'

Twinkle crept out from under the saucepan and everybody watched him anxiously. The wind grew louder and louder and all the tall grasses swayed like trees in the wind. Then there came a sort of voice in the wind and Sandy listened to hear what it said.

'The witches are coming, the witches are coming!' it said, in a deep-down, grumbling sort of voice, rushing into every hole and corner. Sandy peeped through the hole in the saucepan to see what Twinkle was doing. He was dodging here and there between the grasses. At last he reached the place where his red handkerchief lay, and he picked it up and put it into his pocket.

And then, oh my goodness, the pixies in the saucepan saw the first witches coming! They shouted to Twinkle, and he looked up in the sky. There they were, three witches in pointed hats and long cloaks, sitting on long broomsticks, flying through the cloudy sky.

'Quick, Twinkle, quick!' yelled Sandy and the pixies. How they hoped the witches wouldn't see him! He crouched down under a yellow buttercup till they were past, and then began to run to the saucepan.

'There's two more witches coming!' shouted the pixies, pointing. Sure enough, two more could be seen in the windy sky, much lower down than the others. Twinkle crept under a green stinging-nettle and stayed there without a movement till the witches had gone safely by.

'Poor Twinkle! He *will* be stung!' said Gobbo sadly. When the two witches were past Twinkle ran from beneath the nettle straight to the saucepan and crept underneath in safety. How glad all the pixies were! They crowded round him and stroked his nettle-stung hands and face.

'Never mind, Twinkle, you're safe here,' they said.

'Look at all the witches now!' cried Sandy peeping through the hole. 'Oh my! What a wonderful sight! I'm glad I'm seeing this.'

It certainly was a marvellous sight! The sky was simply full of flying witches, and some of them had black cats sitting behind them on the broomsticks. The cats coiled their tails round the sticks and held on like monkeys. It was funny to see them.

'Does this always happen at thirteen o'clock?' asked Sandy.

'Always,' said Twinkle, solemnly. 'But thirteen o'clock only happens once in a blue moon, as I told you before. The moon must have been blue this month. Did you notice it?'

'Well, no, I didn't,' said Sandy. 'I'm nearly always in bed when it's moonlight. Oh, I say! Look! One of the witches has lost her black cat!'

The pixies peeped out of the hole in the saucepan. Sure enough, one of the black cats had tumbled off its broomstick. It had tried to be clever and wash itself on the broomstick, and had lost its hold and tumbled off. It was falling through the air, and the witch was darting down with her broomstick, trying her best to catch it.

She just managed to grab hold of the

# Thirteen O'clock

cat before it fell on the ground – but her broomstick was smashed to pieces, and the witch rolled over and over on the grass, holding the cat safely in her arms. She sat up and looked round. When she saw her broken broomstick she began to howl.

'It's broken. It's broken! I'll never be able to fly back home! Boo hoo hoo!'

Sandy was frightened to see the witch rolling over and over. He thought she would be sure to hurt herself. He was a very kind-hearted boy, and he longed to go and ask her if she was all right. He began to squeeze himself under the saucepan, meaning to go and see if the witch was hurt.

But the pixies tried to pull him back.

'Don't go, don't go,' they whispered, for the witch was quite near. 'She'll change you into a black-beetle.'

'Why should she?' asked Sandy. 'I'm going to be kind to her. Besides, she's got a nice face, rather like my grannie's – I'm sure she isn't a bad witch.'

He wriggled himself away from the

hands of the pixies and ran over to the witch. She was sitting down on the grass crying big tears all down her cheeks. The cat was on her lap, still looking frightened.

The witch was most surprised to see him. Sandy stopped just by her. She had a very tall pointed hat, and a long cloak round her shoulders, with silver suns, moons and stars all over it. The cat arched its back and spat angrily at the little boy.

'Excuse me,' said Sandy, politely. 'I saw you roll over on the ground when your broomstick broke, and I came to see if you were hurt.'

'Well,' said the witch, holding out her left hand, 'I'm not much hurt – but my hand is a bit cut. I must have hit it against a stone when I rolled over.'

'I'll tie it up for you with my handkerchief,' said Sandy. 'It's quite clean.'

The witch looked more astonished than ever. She held out her hand and Sandy tied it up very neatly.

'Thank you,' said the witch. 'That's most kind of you. Oh dear – just look at my poor broomstick – it's broken in half! I shall never get back to Witchland again!'

Sandy looked at the broomstick. The broom part was all right, but the stick was broken. Sandy felt in his pocket to see if he had brought his knife with him. Yes, he had!

'I'll cut you another stick from the

hedge,' he said. 'Then you can fit it into the broom-head and use it to fly away with!'

'You're the cleverest, kindest boy I ever met!' said the witch. 'Thank you so much! Most people are afraid of witches, you know, because they think we will change them into black-beetles, or something – but that's an old-fashioned idea. The old witches *were* like that – but nowadays we witches are decent folk, making magic spells that will do no one any harm at all.'

'Well, I'm glad to hear *that*!' said Sandy, hoping that the pixies under the saucepan were hearing it, too. He went to the hedge and cut another stick for the witch. He fitted it neatly into the broom-head and threw away the broken stick. The witch was very pleased.

She said a magic spell over it to make it able to fly. Then she turned to Sandy.

'Won't you have a ride with me?' she asked. 'It is great fun. I will see that you are safe.'

'Ooh, I'd *love* a ride!' cried Sandy, in delight. 'But you are sure you won't take me away to Witchland?'

'I told you that witches don't do horrid things now,' said the witch. 'Do I *look* like a nasty witch?'

'No, you don't,' said Sandy. 'Well, I'll come for a ride – I'd love to! I'll be awfully late for my dinner but an adventure like this doesn't come often!'

He perched himself on the broomstick, behind the witch, who took her black cat on her knee. Just as they were about to set off, there came a great clatter, and the saucepan nearby was overturned by the pixies. They streamed out, shouting and calling.

'Take us for a ride, too! Take us for a ride, too!'

The witch looked at them in amazement. She had had no idea that any pixies were near. She laughed when she saw where they had been hiding.

'Climb up on the stick,' she said. 'I'll give you a ride too!'

Goodness, there wasn't room to put a

blade of grass on that broomstick after all the pixies had climbed up on it! What a squash there was, to be sure!

The witch called out a string of magic words and the broomstick suddenly flew up into the air with a jerk. Sandy held on tightly. The pixies yelled in delight and began to sing joyfully. All the other witches flying by in the sky laughed to see such a crowded broomstick. Sandy did enjoy himself. He was very high up, and the wind whistled in his ears and blew his hair straight back from his head.

'Now we're going down again!' said the witch, and the broomstick swooped downwards. It landed gently and all the pixies tumbled off in a heap. Sandy jumped off and thanked the witch very much for such a lovely ride.

'I must go now,' she said. 'The hour of thirteen o'clock is nearly over and I must return to Witchland. Goodbye, kind little boy, and I'll give you another ride next time it's thirteen o'clock. If you wait for me here, I'll take you all the way to Witchland and back!'

Off she went, she and her black cat, and left Sandy standing in the grass, watching her fly away. The pixies waved to the witch and she waved back.

'Well, that *was* an adventure!' cried the pixies. 'We'll never be afraid of witches again, that's certain! Hurray!'

'I wonder what the time is,' said

Sandy. 'What comes after thirteen o'clock? Is it fourteen o'clock?'

'Oh no!' said Twinkle. 'Thirteen o'clock just comes and goes. It isn't any time really. It always comes after twelve o'clock, but it's followed by one o'clock as if nothing had happened in between!'

Somewhere a church clock chimed the hour. Sandy listened. Then the clock struck one, and no more.

'One o'clock, one o'clock!' cried the pixies their voices growing small and faint. 'Thirteen o'clock is over! Goodbye, goodbye!'

Sandy looked at them – they were vanishing like mist, and in a moment or two he could see nothing of them. They just weren't there.

'I must make myself big again,' he thought. He remembered the words quite well. He shut his eyes and covered up his ears. He had to say the magic words backwards, so he thought hard before he spoke.

'Pie-allo-looki-hoona!' he said. When

he opened his eyes he was his own size again! He set off home, running as fast as he could, for he was afraid that his mother would be wondering where he was.

He ran into the house and found his mother just putting out his dinner. She didn't seem to think he was late at all!

'You're just in nice time,' she said to Sandy. 'Good boy! You must have come straight from school without stopping!'

'But mother - ever such a lot has happened since I left school,' said Sandy, in surprise. 'I'm dreadfully late!'

'No, darling, it's only just gone one o'clock,' said his mother, looking at the clock.

'Didn't *you* have thirteen o'clock too,

this morning?' asked Sandy, sitting down to his dinner.

'What *are* you talking about?' said his mother with a laugh. 'Thirteen o'clock! Whoever heard of that? That only happens in Fairyland, once in a blue moon, I should think!'

Sandy thought about it. Perhaps it was true – perhaps thirteen o'clock belonged to the fairies, and not to the world of boys and girls. How lucky he had been to have that one magic hour of thirteen o'clock with the pixies and the witch. And next time it was thirteen o'clock he was going to ride on a broomstick again. Oh, what fun!

'I do hope it will be thirteen o'clock again soon,' he said.

'Eat up your dinner and don't talk nonsense!' said his mother, laughing.

But it wasn't nonsense, was it? Sandy is going to blow all the dandelion clocks he sees so that he will know when it is thirteen o'clock again. If you blow them too, you may find that magic hour as well!

# 4

## *The Little Toy Stove*

Angela had a little toy stove. It was a dear little stove, with an oven that had two doors, and three rings at the top to put kettles or saucepans on. At the back was a shelf to warm plates or keep the dinner hot. Angela liked it very much.

But her mother wouldn't let her cook anything on her stove. 'No, Angela,' she said; 'you are not big enough. I am afraid you would burn yourself if you lit the stove and tried to cook something.'

'Oh, but Mummy, it isn't any fun unless I can cook myself something!' said Angela, nearly crying. But Mummy wouldn't let her light the stove, so it was no use saying any more.

Now one day, as Angela was playing with her saucepans and kettles in the garden, filling them with bits of grass for vegetables, and little berries for potatoes and apples, pretending to cook them all for dinner, she heard a tiny voice calling to her.

'Angela! Angela! Do you think you would mind lending me your stove for this evening? My stove has gone wrong, and I have a party. I simply *must* cook for my guests, and so I wondered if you'd lend me *your* stove!'

Angela looked all round to see who was speaking. At last she saw a tiny elf, not more than six inches high, peeping at her from behind a flower.

'Oh!' said Angela in delight. 'I've

never seen a fairy before. Do come and let me look at you.'

The elf ran out from behind the flower. She was dressed in blue and silver, and had long shining wings and a tiny pointed face. Angela thought she was lovely.

'Will you lend me your stove?' asked the elf. 'Please say yes.'

'Of course!' said Angela. 'I'd love to. Will you really cook on it? My mother won't let me.'

'Of course she won't let you,' said the elf. 'You aren't big enough yet. You might burn yourself.'

'Shall I leave my stove here for you?' asked Angela.

'Yes, please,' said the elf. 'I can easily cook out here. It is to be an open-air party. I live behind those big hollyhocks, so I shan't have far to bring my things.'

'I suppose I couldn't come and watch you?' said Angela longingly. 'I've never seen my toy stove really doing cooking, you know!'

# The Little Toy Stove

'Well, you come and watch tonight,' said the elf. 'I shall begin my cooking at nine o'clock. The party begins at eleven.'

Angela was so excited when she went to bed. She meant to put on her dressing-gown and get up at nine o'clock, and creep down the garden. So she lay awake until she heard the hall clock chime nine. Then up she got and slipped down the stairs and out of the garden door.

She could see where her toy stove was quite well, because smoke was rising from it. The elf had got it going well. A lovely smell of baking and roasting came on the air. Oooh!

You should have seen the elf cooking on that stove. The oven was full of things roasting away well. The saucepans were full of delicious fruits and vegetables!

'Just listen to my pudding boiling away in that saucepan,' said the elf, pleased. 'This stove cooks very well indeed, it's a fine stove.'

'What sort of pudding is it?' asked Angela.

'It's a tippy-top pudding,' said the elf. 'And I'm cooking a poppity cake too and some google buns.'

'Oh my, they do sound delicious,' said Angela; 'and so exciting! I've never heard of them before. I suppose I couldn't come to the party?'

'No,' said the elf. 'It is too late a party for little girls like you. But, Angela, as I think it is really very kind of you to let

71

me use your lovely stove for my cooking, I'd like you to taste some of my dishes. Listen! There is sure to be some tippy-top pudding, some poppity cake, and a few google buns over after the party. If there are I will put them on a plate and leave them inside the oven. See? I will clean the stove nicely, too, and leave it all shiny and bright. Now, good night, dear. You must go to bed. You are yawning.'

'Good night!' said Angela, and she ran off. In the morning she went to see if there *was* anything inside her oven. And what do you think? There was a neat little blue dish, and on one side of it was a slice of yellow tippy-top pudding, and on the other side were three google buns, red and blue, and a large slice of green poppity cake! Ooooh!

Angela ate them all – and they were simply delicious. She *does* hope the elf will want to borrow her stove again. Wouldn't it be lovely if she did?

# 5

## *The Beautiful Cricket Ball*

The boys were going to play cricket.
There were the twins, Peter, and John,
Alec, Tom, Jim, Fred, Ian, and Hugh.
What fun it would be!

'We will play on that nice smooth
stretch of sand!' said Peter. 'You put
the stumps in, John!'

Little Harry came running up. 'Peter,
Peter!' he cried. 'Can I play too!'

'No,' said Peter. 'You're too small.'

'But I can run fast,' said Harry. 'Oh,
do let me play, Peter. I won't ask to bat
- just let me field for you.'

'No, we've got enough players,' said Peter. 'Run along and play with your sister, Harry.'

Harry was very disappointed. He had so hoped to play cricket with the big boys. It would have been such fun. He could run very fast, and although he didn't bat very well, he could bowl quite straight.

He went off, hurt and sad. Peter might have given him a chance!

His little sister was building a castle. 'Come and help, Harry,' she said. Harry took up his spade and began to dig. It was no good being horrid to Susan just because someone had been horrid to *him*!

The boys drove in the stumps – and then Fred brought out a most beautiful new cricket ball.

'Look, boys,' he said. 'Here's a fine ball! I had it for my birthday yesterday!'

'My!' said Peter and the others, looking at the beautiful ball admiringly. 'That's a beauty! Can we play with it today, Fred?'

'Yes,' said Fred, proudly. 'But will you let me bat first if I let you play with my new ball?'

'All right,' said the others. 'Take the bat, Fred. Who's going to bowl? You, John! See if you can get Fred out with his own ball!'

The game began. Harry, still digging castles, could hear the click of the ball against the bat as Fred drove it over the sand and then ran. The boys shouted. They ran after the ball and threw it in. John stopped bowling and Ian began. It all looked very jolly indeed, and Harry wished and wished he could have played too.

At last Fred was bowled out. He gave up the bat to Peter, who was a very good batsman indeed. Hugh took the fine new ball to bowl to Peter. It felt so good as he twirled it about – the best ball the boys had ever had to play with!

Hugh bowled, and Peter struck out. The ball flew along the sand, and Peter ran, and ran and ran. He meant to make more runs than anyone else that morning! At last the ball was thrown in again and Hugh caught it. He bowled it to Peter again.

Peter slashed out with the bat. Click! went the ball. The ball flew towards the rocks.

'Stop it, Ian, stop it!' yelled Fred. 'Don't let it go among the rocks, or we shall lose it.'

But Ian could not stop it, for the ball was going too fast. It rolled straight towards the rocks. It struck one and flew up into the air – then it dropped somewhere.

'Find it, find it, Ian!' yelled everyone. 'Hurry! Peter is making more runs than anyone!'

Ian hunted round the rocks. He could not see the ball anywhere. How he hunted! He looked under the seaweed. He looked in every pool. That beautiful new ball was not to be seen!

At last the others came to help him look too. They peered here and there, they splashed into all the pools, but it wasn't a bit of good – that ball could *not* be found!

'It's gone,' said Fred, very much upset. 'Quite disappeared. What shall we do?'

'Better play with our old one,' said John. So the old one was got out and the game went on. But everyone was very sad about Fred's fine new ball. It was too bad to lose it the very first game.

Harry had been digging all the time the boys were hunting for the ball. He didn't like to go near them, for he was afraid they would send him away again. He did not know whether they had found the ball or not – but when he saw them playing again he thought they must have found their ball. He didn't know it was the old one.

The castle was finished at last. Susan wanted to do something else. 'Let's go shrimping,' she said.

'All right,' said Harry. 'We'll catch some shrimps for your tea, Susan.'

They took their shrimping nets and went to the rock-pools. They pushed their nets through the sand and looked to see how many shrimps they had caught.

'Only one tiny crab,' said Susan, and she and Harry put their nets into the water again.

'I can see a big prawn!' suddenly shouted Harry, in delight. 'Hurrah! Come here into my net, prawn!'

But the prawn would not be caught. He darted here and there, and at last disappeared under a shelving rock that jutted out into the pool. Harry stuck his net under the rock to catch the prawn.

He drew his net out and looked into it – no – there was no prawn there!

'Harry, something rolled out from under that rock when you stuck your net there,' said Susan, pointing. 'What was it?'

Harry looked down into the pool. He saw a big red ball there. He picked it up. 'It must have been under that ledge or rock,' he said. 'And when I poked my

net underneath it must have made the ball roll out. I wonder whose ball it is.'

'It belongs to those boys,' said Susan. 'I heard them say they hadn't found their ball. They are playing with another one.'

'Are they really, Susan?' said Harry. 'This must be Fred's beautiful new ball then. He must have been upset when it couldn't be found.'

'Are you going to take it back to them?' asked Susan.

'I don't know,' said Harry. 'They were horrid to me this morning. I don't see why I should be nice to them.'

'But Fred will be so sad if he doesn't get his new ball back,' said kind-hearted Susan. 'Don't you remember how bad we felt when we lost our new kite, Harry?'

'Yes,' said Harry. 'All right, I'll take it back to the boys.'

He dried the ball on a towel, and then ran to where the boys were playing. He waited until the batsman was bowled out and then he yelled to Peter:

'Peter! I've found Fred's new ball! It was in the rock-pool, catch!'

The boys turned in surprise. Fred gave a cheer. 'Hurrah! I'm so glad!'

Peter caught the ball and stared at Harry. 'That's jolly good of you,' he said. 'You are a sport! I say, boys, what about letting him come into the game? He must be a good sort to bring back our ball when we wouldn't let him play this morning!'

'Yes, let him come!' roared all the boys. 'Come on, young Harry! We'll let you play with us. It was kind of you to give back our ball!'

So Harry joined the game – and wasn't he pleased and proud. He fields very well indeed, and do you know, although he only made one run, he bowled out Ian and Hugh. The boys were quite surprised.

'You play a good game, Harry,' said Peter, at the end. 'You can come and play with us again tomorrow.'

Now Harry always plays cricket with the big boys – and how glad he is that he took Susan's advice and was nice to the boys when he really didn't want to be! As for Fred's beautiful new ball, they are still playing with it. Its stay in the rock-pool didn't hurt it a bit!

# 6

## *The Naughty Sailor Doll*

Tilda, the little brown-haired doll, had a pretty green brooch. It had come out of a Christmas cracker and Peggy had given it to Tilda because she was her favourite doll.

Tilda loved the brooch and was very proud of it. She always wore it on her frock – and then one day she lost it! She was so upset.

'It *must* be somewhere in the nursery!'

But the sailor doll wouldn't. Then the toys hunted and hunted all over the nursery once more but still they couldn't find that brooch anywhere. It was most annoying.

The sailor doll sat himself in his corner and grinned at the toys. He was very naughty.

The toys held a meeting at the back of the toy cupboard to plan what to do. Nobody could think of anything at all – and then suddenly the little mouse, who lived in the wall, popped his head in.

'I heard you talking about that bad sailor doll,' he said. 'I have a plan. Shall I tell it to you?'

'Oh yes, do!' cried the toys.

'Well,' said the little mouse, 'tonight, when everything is dark and still, I will creep out of my hole. I will run on my soft tippy-toes to the sailor doll – *and I will take away the clockwork key out of his leg!*'

The toys thought it was a wonderful plan.

'He won't be able to wind himself up and run about any more!' said Tilda. 'Then perhaps he will tell us where he has hidden my brooch! It's a fine plan, mouse!'

So that night, just before dawn, when all was still and dark, the little brown mouse crept out of his hole and ran over to where the sailor doll slept in his corner. He took the clockwork key in his mouth and pulled gently. It came out of the doll's leg, and the mouse ran back to his hole with it, squeaking with delight.

Next morning the toys looked across at the sailor doll. He had no key to wind himself up with! At first he didn't notice the key was gone – but when he bent down to wind himself up so that he might go for a run round the nursery he found there was no key to wind with!

He stared in dismay. Whatever had happened to his key? He couldn't walk unless he was wound up – and how could he wind himself up with no key?

He shouted angrily to the toys.

'Where is my key? Have you taken it?'

'Not one of us toys has touched it!' said the brown teddy bear.

'Well, where has it gone, then?' asked the sailor doll, looking all round for the key. Nobody said a word.

'You might help me to look for it,' grumbled the sailor doll.

'Why should we?' asked Tilda. 'You wouldn't help us look for my brooch. Tell us where you have put my brooch and perhaps we will tell you where your key is.'

The sailor doll sulked and sulked. The toys played together and took no notice of him. At last he could bear it no longer.

'You'll find Tilda's brooch in the toy teapot,' he said. 'That's where I hid it.'

Sure enough it was there! Tilda took it out of the toy teapot and proudly pinned it on her frock again. Then they called the little brown mouse from his hole.

'The sailor doll has told us where the brooch was,' said Tilda. 'Now you can tell him where his key is.'

'*I've* got it!' said the mouse to the surprised sailor doll. 'But I shan't give it you back just yet, because my little baby mice like to play with it. You can wait. You made Tilda wait for her brooch, and now you can wait for your key.'

Then the sailor doll turned red and began to cry.

'I'm sorry I was so wicked,' he sobbed. 'I am a horrid doll. Please forgive me and I'll never do such a thing again.'

So the toys forgave him and that evening the little mouse brought back his key. He fitted it into his leg, wound himself up, and took a fine run round the nursery. He knows the mouse will take away his key if ever he is horrid again – and, as he hasn't once missed it since that day, I expect he must have behaved himself, don't you?

# 7

## *Holes in His Stockings*

Mister Ho-Hhum was a brownie with twinkling eyes and a merry smile. He worked hard and was generous and good-tempered – but there was just one thing he was always forgetting to do; and that was to mend the holes in his stockings.

His friend, Mister Hum-Hho, used to scold Ho-Hhum loudly, when he saw him taking off his shoes in the evening, and spied the enormous holes in the toes and heels of his stockings.

'Ho-Hhum!' he would cry, 'look at that dreadful hole, with your toe poking out! I'm ashamed of you. Why, don't you mend your stockings?'

'It doesn't matter,' Ho-Hhum would say, with a grin. 'Nobody sees them when I walk out. I don't take off my shoes in the street.'

'Well, one day you *might* have to!' said Hum-Hho, 'and then think how dreadful you would feel when everyone saw your toes poking through your stockings. I hope I'm not with you when *that* happens!'

'You needn't worry,' said Ho-Hhum, gaily. 'I shall NEVER take off my shoes in the street, so nobody will EVER see the holes in my stockings!'

And the naughty brownie went on wearing holey stockings every day – till something happened.

One Saturday morning he and Hum-Hho went out for a walk together, for it was a very fine day. They went round by the King's palace, and as they walked they heard the little Prince Peronel playing and shouting in the garden. Then suddenly they heard him cry bitterly.

The two brownies pushed open the garden door and rushed into the palace garden. They saw that the little Prince had tumbled out of his toy motor-car and had bumped his head. One wheel was off the car and lay nearby on the ground.

Ho-Hhum picked up the little boy and wiped his tears. Hum-Hho picked up the motor-car. Prince Peronel wept to see the wheel off.

'Now what shall I do?' he cried. 'I can't ride in it!'

'If you've a hammer I could put the wheel on for you,' said Ho-Hhum, kindly.

'I'm not allowed to have a hammer,' said the little Prince. 'But I know what you could do, brownie. Couldn't you take off your big, strong shoe and use that to knock my wheel on with? Oh, couldn't you?'

Mister Ho-Hhum thought he could quite well – and then, oh, my goodness me, he remembered that he had a great big hole in each of his stockings, and the holes would show dreadfully if he took his shoes off. Then what would the Prince think? He might even tell the King and Queen about the brownie that had holes in his stockings.

So he shook his head.

'No,' he said. 'I can't use one of my shoes. I'll use a stone instead.'

So he picked up a stone and tried to knock the wheel on with that. But the stone broke to pieces and a little bit flew off and cut the Prince's hand. He began to cry again and the two brownies were terribly upset.

'Why didn't you use your shoe as the Prince asked you?' said Hum-Hho to Ho-Hhum, quite forgetting that his friend had dreadful holes in his stockings. 'Don't cry, little Prince. I'll knock the wheel on with one of *my* shoes!'

So Hum-Hho quickly slipped off one of his shoes and in a trice he had knocked the wheel on to the toy motor-car and mended it! Peronel was delighted. He jumped in and rode down the path, calling loudly:

'Nurse! Mother! A kind brownie has mended my motor for me! Can he come to tea?'

Then, to the brownie's great surprise who should come running down the path but the Fairy Queen herself, all in silver, shining like the moon. She kissed the little Prince and listened to what he had to say.

'I want this brownie to come to tea with me,' he said, taking hold of Hum-Hho's hand. 'Not the other one. He's unkind. He wouldn't take his shoe off and mend my wheel for me. But this one did.'

Poor Ho-Hhum! He turned very red and ran out of the garden as fast as he could. As for Hum-Hho, he was so pleased at being asked to tea at the palace that he could hardly say a word!

Off he went with the little Prince and had a lovely time. When he got home again, he called at Ho-Hhum's house to tell him all about it.

And what was Ho-Hhum doing? Do you know? Of course you do! He was sitting on a stool, and round him were nine pairs of stockings, all with holes in – and Ho-Hhum was mending them as fast as he could.

'Don't scold me, Hum-Hho!' he cried, when he saw his friend. 'I couldn't take my shoe off to mend that wheel because of the dreadful holes in my stocking. And now I am *never* going to have holey stockings again. Oh, how ashamed I felt to think I couldn't help the Prince!'

And two big tears rolled on to his darning-needle. Poor Ho-Hhum! Never mind, he has never had a hole in his stockings since that day!

222  8070

# 8

# *He Didn't Believe in Fairies*

There was once a farmer who didn't believe in fairies. You should have heard him laugh when fairies were mentioned! Why, he almost deafened you!

Now I expect you have heard it said that only those who believe in the Little Folk ever see them. Those who *don't* believe in them can't see them even when they are right under their noses! And often the fairies play tricks on these people just to teach them.

Farmer Straw only believed in horses, cows, sheep and things like that. If you mentioned such things as dragons, unicorns, witches or pixies he would

102

explode with laughter and call you a ninny. The fairy folk used to listen, and they laughed too. It really *was* funny to them, you see, to think that people said they weren't there, when *they* knew quite well they were!

Now Farmer Straw had a very fine mushroom field. So had his neighbour, Farmer Twinkle, and his other neighbour, Dame Busy. And in the autumn they all got up very early in the mornings and went mushrooming.

103

When they sold their mushrooms in the market they made a great deal of money.

One night the little folk had had a dance in Dame Busy's field. It was a GRAND dance, with the grasshopper band playing rilloby-rill half the evening. That is the famous elfin tune, you know, that the grasshoppers know so well. There had been all kinds of games too, and a most delicious feast. And for once it hadn't ended at cock-crow, but just a little bit later.

Now this was a pity – because no sooner did the party break up than a rainstorm began! How it poured! How it pelted! The fairies, pixies and elves raced for the shelter of the mushrooms that had shot up in the night. They crouched beneath them and tried to keep their lovely frocks from being splashed. They hoped the rain would soon stop.

But it didn't. No, it went on and on and on. Goodness, the little folk couldn't possibly go home in it, they would be wet through! And see – there were lights in the farm-houses! People were getting up early to go mushrooming. Then what would happen to the fairies?

Dame Busy came out of her farm-house with a big basket.

'Hey, little folk!' cried an elf. 'We shall be caught here if Dame Busy arrives before we go. She believes in fairies, you know, so she'll see us here under the mushrooms. Let us quickly run to the mushrooms in the other field – those belonging to Farmer Twinkle.'

So off the fairy folk scuttled through the wet grass and the rain, and soon they were safely sheltering under Farmer Twinkle's mushrooms. But dear

me – it wasn't long before the farmer opened *his* farm-house door and came out to go mushrooming too!

So off went the fairies again – this time to Farmer Straw's mushrooms. And bother me if *his* door didn't open and out he came too, to go mushrooming!

'Our luck is out this morning!' cried an elf. 'Whatever can we do? There are no more mushrooms to shelter us from this dreadful rainstorm! We shall have to go home and oh dear, what colds we shall get, for we shall be soaked through!'

'No, don't let's get wet!' cried a pixie. 'There's no need to! Let's each pick our mushroom and use it like the humans use umbrellas! We can carry them all the way home and never get wet at all! As for old Farmer Straw he won't see us for he doesn't believe in fairies! Ho ho!'

'Ho ho ho ho!' laughed all the little folk delightedly. Then they each picked a mushroom, and holding it above their bright little heads they made their way across the wet field down to the little wood where they lived.

Farmer Straw met them as he came to the field with his basket – yes, he met them – but he couldn't see the fairies, of course, because he didn't believe in them! All he saw was a row of big mushrooms walking solemnly along in the rain! He stood and stared with his mouth wide open. Then he gave a scream of fright and ran back to his farm.

'Oh! Oh! I'm going mad! I've seen mushrooms walking! Oh, what shall I do?'

'Don't be so silly!' shouted Dame Busy and Farmer Twinkle. 'It's only the little folk using them as umbrellas!'

'I don't believe in the fairies!' yelled Farmer Straw. 'No, that I don't.'

'Oh well, if you like to believe in mushrooms walking off by themselves, instead of in the little folk, you do as you like,' said Dame Busy, scornfully. 'But it seems to me to be much easier to believe in fairies than in walking mushrooms!'

Farmer Straw looked back at the row of bobbing mushrooms, half-believing in the little folk for a moment – and just for that moment he saw a roguish face peeping at him from under a mushroom and caught the glint of a silvery pair of wings. But it was gone in a flash.

'Only ninnies believe in fairies,' he said. 'I'm not a ninny. There's some-

# He Didn't Believe in Fairies

thing gone wrong with my eyes this morning, that's all - or else I'm not properly awake yet. Ho - I'd rather believe in walking mushrooms than a dozen fairies! That I would!'

But I wouldn't. Would you? Anyway, Farmer Straw lost all his mushrooms that day and you should have heard the little folk laugh about it! Farmer Straw thought it was the swallows twittering - but it wasn't.

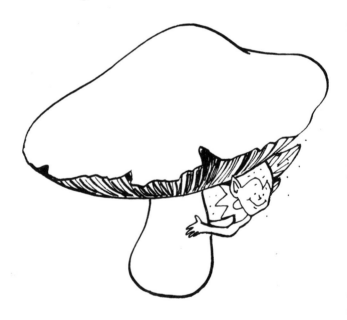

# 9

## *Big-Eyes the Enchanter*

Big-eyes the Enchanter had found a most marvellous spell. It was made of moonshine, starlight, the roots of mountains, the footfalls of a weasel, the breath of a fish and the smell of rain. It was stirred up with a Hoodle-Bird's tail-feather and boiled on a piece of shining ice.

It was the most powerful spell in the world. It would make Big-Eyes the Enchanter King of all the Lands on Earth. He could do what he liked. Ah, what a time he would have!

Big-Eyes was not a pleasant fellow. He didn't like flowers, he didn't like animals, he hated children. He couldn't bear fairies, he spanked every elf he met, and he hated to hear anyone laughing.

'When I use my spell and make myself King of all the Lands on Earth, I will destroy the flowers everywhere!' he cried. 'I will shut all the animals up underground, and I will make all the boys and girls work hard for me from the moment they are three years old. As for the fairies and the elves, the goblins and the pixies, I'll send the whole lot to the bottom of the sea. Ho, what a time I'll have!'

He looked at the spell. It was shimmering in a great blue cauldron, stirred by his servant, a big lad with a stupid, grinning face.

Then Big-Eyes looked in his book of magic. He wanted to find out exactly when the spell would work. At last he found what he wanted to know.

'This spell when made will only act on Midsummer Day at five o'clock in the morning,' he read. 'Aha! Then I'll set my alarm clock for half-past four, and get the spell working at five exactly. Then thunder and lightning will come and when the spell has

stopped everyone will be my slave!'

The night before Midsummer Day the Enchanter set his alarm clock to go off at half-past four. Then he went to bed, full of excitement to think of all the power that would be his next day. His servant, the grinning lad, had been told to keep awake all night, and stir the spell to keep it sweet.

The Enchanter had exciting dreams. He dreamt that he was a monarch on a golden throne, set with all the rare

113

jewels of the world. He dreamt that not a single flower blossomed on the earth. He dreamt that all the puppies and kittens, chicks and ducklings, calves and lambs were hidden away from the sunshine deep in the heart of the earth. He dreamt that all the boys and girls no longer played but worked all day long for him.

Sweet dreams for the wicked Enchanter! On he dreamt and on – and at last woke up. No alarm bell woke him –

he woke up himself. He looked at the clock. It was half-past three.

Not time to get up yet. He lay and waited. Then he looked at the clock again, when about half an hour had gone.

It was still half-past three. What a strange thing! The Enchanter listened for a moment – and he could hear no ticking! The clock had stopped at half-past three in the morning. He had forgotten to wind it up in his excitement the night before!

The village clock began to strike outside. One-two-three-four-five-six! Six o'clock! The right minute for the working of the spell was past! It wouldn't come again until a year was past!

In a fearful rage the enchanter sprang out of bed. Why hadn't the servant lad warned him, when the clock had stopped? He was supposed to keep awake all night and stir the blue cauldron!

The boy was fast asleep, poor lad, his

head resting on the cauldron. Big-Eyes took him by the shoulder and shook him in fury. The boy woke up in fright, and, thinking that the Enchanter was a thief come in the night, he struck out with all his might.

Biff! The Enchanter fell to the ground, and as he fell he caught at the cauldron to save himself. Sizzle-sizzle-sizzle! The shimmering spell inside upset all over him as he lay on the ground.

The servant lad watched in terror. What would his master do to him now? He would beat him, surely, or at least turn him into a frog or beetle.

The spell acted strangely. It altered the Enchanter bit by bit. He changed slowly into an old man – an old ragged man with a long ragged beard and bald head. He became a beggar-man, and slowly rose from the ground and went out to stand at a corner to beg from the passers-by. And little children were sorry for him and gave him pennies.

Sometimes he remembered how he had been a great Enchanter, and then

he would shake his head and mutter: 'Ah! I could have ruled the world! But I forgot to wind up the clock!'

As for the servant lad, what became of him? He got such a terrible fright that he ran off to sea, and one day he told this story to me. At the end he shook his head and said: 'Ah, it was a good thing my master forgot to wind up his clock that night!'

And dear me, I think it was too!

# 10

## *The Clever Toy Drum*

Nobody in the toy cupboard liked the toy drum. For one thing it was rather big and took up a lot of room. And for another thing it made such a noise when the drumsticks beat on the drum that all the dolls and animals were quite deafened.

'It's a noisy thing, that drum,' said the rabbit.

'It's too big for the toy cupboard,' said the white teddy bear. 'I shan't let it sleep here at night. I shall push it out on to the carpet!'

The white teddy bear was quite bold enough to do this, but the drum didn't wait to be pushed. Every night it quietly rolled itself out of the cupboard on to the carpet so as to give the toys

more room, and stayed there all by itself. It was sad and lonely, for a drum likes jolly friends and chattering and noise – but it wouldn't push itself where it wasn't wanted.

'After all, I can't help being a drum,' it thought, puzzled. 'I might have been a trumpet, or a rabbit or even a white teddy bear. But I was made into a drum, and a drum must be round and it must make a noise.'

Sometimes the drum tried to talk to

Lucy Ann, the little golden-haired doll in the blue dress, who sat on a pretty chair just inside the toy cupboard. Lucy Ann didn't really mind the drum, but she pretended to be as grand as the others, and when the drum murmured a few words to her she turned her pretty back on it and wouldn't answer.

Then one night the toys decided to have a party. But they didn't ask the drum. Oh no! He was left out as usual. There were to be cakes, sandwiches and sweets, and afterwards the musical box had promised to play so that the toys could dance. It would be a lovely party.

And then the toys discovered that they hadn't a doll's table big enough to put all the dishes on! So what do you think they did? Why, they pushed the drum into the middle of the nursery floor, whisked a white table-cloth over him, and used him for a table!

They never even asked him if they might. He would do for a table, so he must put up with it, they thought. They giggled when they thought of him, sitting quietly under the table-cloth, holding all the lovely things to eat. Silly old drum! Only Lucy Ann, the golden-haired doll, felt a little bit sorry for him. But she didn't like to say anything.

The drum was so surprised when it felt the cloth whisked over him and the dishes set down on him that he couldn't say a word. He was very angry indeed. It was too bad of the toys! They hadn't even asked him to the party, that was the worst of it. If they had asked him, he would have been pleased to help them and be their table – but they were unkind and they treated him as if he hadn't any feelings at all.

The drum had half a mind to get up and roll away, cloth, dishes and all! That would upset the toys finely and spoil their party! All the cakes would go rolling on to the floor, all the sandwiches would be upset. The drum really thought he would do it.

Then he thought of Lucy Ann.

Perhaps she would cry if he played such an unkind trick. She wasn't very nice to him, but she was so pretty and so sweet that the drum was really very fond of her. So he stayed still and let the toys use him for their table.

Now just as they were in the middle of their party, the nursery door was pushed open, and in came Scamp the puppy! He had smelt the cakes and sandwiches and had come to see where they were. When he saw the toys there, sitting round the drum-table, eating, he was surprised. He bounded up to them and tried to push them away with his nose.

The toys jumped up, screaming. They took up the dishes of cakes and plates of sandwiches and ran into the toy cupboard with them. They knew how greedy the puppy was. They didn't like him a bit.

Scamp was angry when he saw the toys taking away the cakes and sandwiches. He snatched the cloth off the drum to see if there were any cakes under it. Then he ran into the toy cupboard and sniffed about for the sandwiches he knew were hidden there. When he couldn't find them (because the clever rabbit had hidden them in the brick box and shut down the lid) he was angrier than ever.

He took up the rabbit and shook him hard. Then he took the white teddy bear and tore off his nice blue ribbon. After that he nibbled some hair off the biggest doll and bit the tail off the poor frightened plush monkey.

What a to-do there was! The toys were crying and shouting, nearly frightened to death. Lucy Ann crouched in a corner of the cupboard, hoping and hoping that the puppy wouldn't see her. But he did, he dragged her out by her pretty blue frock, and she bumped her head against the toy cupboard.

Now all this time the drum stood outside watching. You might have thought that he would have been glad to see the unkind toys punished like this by the puppy – but he wasn't. No, he was worried and frightened. He didn't like to hear the rabbit crying and he couldn't bear to see the white teddy bear without his nice blue ribbon. It was dreadful. The toy drum felt very sorry for all the toys.

Ah, but when he heard pretty little Lucy Ann, the golden-haired doll, crying in fright when the puppy pulled her out of the toy cupboard, then something happened to the drum. He began to think harder than ever he had in his life before, because he couldn't bear to hear Lucy Ann crying like that.

'I must get help, somehow!' thought the drum, anxiously. 'Oh, how can I get help? It's no use rolling out of the nursery to fetch the children, because they sleep in too high a bed for me to reach them. What can I do?'

Then he had a wonderful idea! He would beat himself with his two drum sticks, and that would surely wake up the children! So up leapt the two drum sticks and began to beat the drum as loudly as they could.

Rub-a-dub-dub! Rub-a-dub-dub! RUB-A-DUB-DUB!

Now Molly and Tony, the two children, were fast asleep in bed when the drum began to beat, for it was night-time and everyone was sleeping. But when the sound of the toy drum came into their dreams they both woke up in a hurry! They knew the sound of the drum very well indeed, for they beat it every day when they played at soldiers.

126

'Listen, Tony,' said Molly. 'That's our drum! What's it sounding for? Let's go and see!'

Out of bed they jumped and ran into the day nursery – and when they had put on the light they saw that rascal of a puppy shaking the toys like rats!

'Oh, you wicked fellow!' said Tony, smacking the puppy hard. 'You know you ought to stay in your basket down in the kitchen all night. Go back to it at once!'

The puppy ran away quickly. The children stood and looked at the drum. It had stopped beating itself as soon as it had heard them coming, and was now quite silent.

'Who beat the drum, I wonder?' said Molly, astonished. 'One of the toys must have done it to waken us.'

'Isn't that strange?' said Tony, sleepily. 'I wonder which toy it was, Molly. Well, we've rescued them from Scamp, so we might as well go back to bed now. I'm so sleepy.'

They went back to bed and left the toys alone. At first they were too upset and too frightened to speak. Then they sat and thought to themselves – and they thought about the clever, kind little drum, that had saved them from that dreadful rough puppy. The drum might have left them all to be nibbled and shaken – but it hadn't. It had called for help. It was a good-hearted drum, and a smart one too.

The rabbit got up first. He went to the drum. 'Please forgive me for having been unkind to you,' he said. 'I'm sorry.'

'So am I,' cried the white teddy bear.

'And so are we!' cried all the rest.

Lucy Ann, the golden-haired doll, ran to the drum and flung her arms around him.

'You're a darling!' she said. 'You're cleverer and kinder than all the rest of us together. You shall be my friend!'

Well, think of that! The drum trembled with delight and didn't know what to say. Then the toys fetched out their cakes and sandwiches and gave another party, this time for the little toy drum. And always after that they were kind to him and made him their friend.

But he still likes pretty little Lucy Ann the best of all.

# 11

## *The Dog Who Would Go Digging*

Pete belonged to Dickie and Joan. He was the jolliest pup in the world, and there was nothing he liked better than having a game with you. He would let you try to catch him, if you liked the game of 'He'. He would rush miles after a ball if you wanted to play 'Ball', and if you just wanted to go for a walk, why, he'd go with you all the way there and back.

So you can guess that the children loved him very much. Mummy thought he was a nice little dog too – and so did Daddy, until one day he caught Pete digging in the garden!

'Hey, you rascal! Come off the beds!'

yelled Daddy. 'How dare you! You're spoiling all the seeds I planted.'

Pete stopped – but as soon as Daddy's back was turned, he was digging again!

You see, he had suddenly discovered that it was good fun to bury the bones he couldn't eat! Then when he felt hungry he could dig them up and gnaw them. But, of course, as he hadn't a very good memory he couldn't always remember where he had buried his bones – so he had to dig here and dig there until at last he found them.

Daddy didn't like him digging here and digging there, for Daddy did the garden. It was Daddy who planted the seeds, and the bulbs, Daddy who carefully planted the little pansy plants, and forget-me-nots and the wallflowers. Daddy loved the garden and spent all his spare time there. So no wonder he was cross when Pete dug everything up!

Then there came a dreadful week, when Pete dug up the garden EVERY day! Yes – he dug up the candytuft seeds; he dug up three nice pansy plants; he dug up all the poppy seedlings that had come up so nicely in one big patch. And worst of all he took it into his silly little head that he had buried a bone underneath Daddy's best rose-tree! So he even dug up the rose-tree!

Daddy got crosser and crosser – and at last he said a dreadful thing.

'Pete must go. I'm not going to spend all my spare time working to make the garden nice, only to have Pete digging it all up every five minutes. If you children can't teach him to be good, I shall give him to the milkman. He wants a dog, I know.'

Oh my goodness! You should have seen poor Joan and Dickie! They went quite pale with fright. How COULD Daddy think of giving their own puppy away to the milkman? Why, they loved him with all their hearts, he was the nicest puppy in the world. They simply couldn't do without him.

'Please, Daddy, don't do that,' said Joan, her eyes full of tears. 'He doesn't mean to dig up your seeds.'

'I don't care if he means to or not,' said Daddy crossly. 'He does it just the same. Anyway, he goes to the milkman next week if he does any more damage.'

Well, Joan and Dickie did their best to make Pete behave – but one evening when they had gone out to play with a friend, Pete dug an enormous hole in the middle of Daddy's row of garden peas, which were JUST coming up.

Daddy spanked the puppy hard and then spoke to Mummy.

'Give him to the milkman on Monday,' he said. 'I'm tired of him, and I'm not going to waste my time doing things that Pete simply undoes the very next minute.'

The children knew it was no good saying anything. When Daddy spoke like that he meant what he said. But how unhappy they were! How wet their pillows were that night! They did so love Pete – he really was such a dear, fat, playful fellow. If only he wouldn't dig up poor Daddy's garden! But it was no use – he had done it once too often and now he must go away.

Sunday came. Daddy took Mummy and the two children out for a bus-ride to see the buttercup fields, which were just like golden carpets then. Pete was left behind. And, of course, in his little doggy mind he thought: 'Ha! A good time for digging! Now where's that bone I buried two days ago?'

He ran into the garden. He found a nice corner under a big old lilac bush, and then began to dig. How he dug! He felt sure the bone was there. He was going to dig until he found it, anyway, even if he dug a hole as big as a house.

Scrape, scrape, scrape, went his strong little paws. Snuffle, snuffle, snuffle, went his nose! Ah! Here was the bone at last! Scrape, scrape, scrape!

What a large bone! Pete didn't re-

## The Dog Who Would Go Digging

member that it was so large when he had buried it. Goodness, it must have grown since he buried it. Well, things grew in the ground – seeds shot up – plants grew – perhaps bones grew as well. Ha, what a fine bone it would be!

Pete panted and puffed, scraped and snuffled – but he couldn't get that bone up. It was too big and too heavy. So he sat down for a rest, his tongue hanging out. And there Daddy and the children found him, when they got home.

'That dog has been digging again!' cried Daddy in a rage. He ran up to the lilac bush, and Pete shot away. He didn't want to be spanked again. Daddy looked into the hole, and then he looked again.

'Is it one of Pete's bones?' asked Joan, sorry that the puppy should have behaved badly again. 'Oh Daddy! It's not a bone! It's a funny old box! Look, Pete has got one end out – but it was too big for him to get right out! I expect he thought it was a very big bone!'

'Whatever is it?' asked Dickie, excitedly. 'Quick, Daddy, get it up!'

Daddy was red with excitement too. Whatever could the box be? He fetched his spade and began to dig it up. At last he and Dickie lifted it up on to the grass – and then Joan cried out in surprise.

'Oh! It's got our name on it – look – it says PAGET. That's our name, isn't it, Daddy? You're Mr Paget and Mummy's Mrs Paget. Why is it on this old box?'

'My dears,' said Daddy, still red with

excitement, 'my dears, I BELIEVE it must be the box of jewels belonging to your great-grandmother, who lived in this same house. They were stolen by a burglar and never found again. He must have buried them in the garden, and then never had the chance to get them again.'

Well, Daddy was right! You should have seen the lovely things in that box! Great-Grandma had been a beauty and had had wonderful necklaces, bracelets and brooches. Some Daddy said he would keep for Mummy and Joan – others he would sell, and they would bring a lot of money.

How the children clapped their hands! How Mummy cried out for joy to see the pretty things! What excitement to find treasure like that, hidden for so many years!

Nobody thought of Pete, who had found it quite by mistake.

Pete heard the excitement and he longed to join in it. He put his little nose round the door and said 'Wuff!' in a small, quiet voice, in case Daddy was still angry with him.

But Daddy wasn't. Dear me no! Pete had really done some good with his digging this time, so there was no scolding for him, only petting and lots of biscuits.

'You won't give him to the milkman now, will you, Daddy?' asked Joan, hugging the puppy tightly.

'No,' said Daddy. 'He's not a bad little chap. And besides, if he digs up the garden any more we shall be able to afford a gardener to put the damage right, with all the money that will come from these jewels!'

'WUFF WUFF!' barked Pete, joyfully. And wasn't it a very funny thing – he never in his life dug in the garden again! Joan said he must have been digging for the treasure all the time, and so of course, stopped digging when he found it. Mummy says he must have had enough of digging, and decided to be a grown-up dog. What do *you* think?

# 12

## *Dame Thimble and Her Matches*

There was once an old woman called Dame Thimble who lit her lamp as soon as it got dark each night. And every night she had to hunt for her matches.

Sometimes they were on the mantelpiece, sometimes they were on the dresser, sometimes they were in the kitchen drawer and most often they were in the cupboard.

But, of course, it is hard to find matches when it is dark, and Dame Thimble bumped herself so often trying to find them that she decided to do something about it.

'I'll put them in my pocket in the morning,' she said, 'then when the

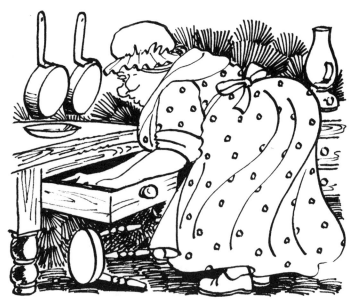

evening comes I shall just have to put my hand in my pocket, and there I shall find the matches as easily as anything! I can light my lamp at once without hunting all over the place first!'

So in the morning she put the matches in her pocket, and then busied herself with her day's washing and ironing. She worked hard until tea-time, when she sat down and had a nice cup of tea. After tea she had to wash up, and as it was getting very dark by then, she wanted to light her lamp.

So she went to the cupboard to find her matches. They weren't there. Then she went to the kitchen dresser, but they weren't there either. Then she felt all along the mantelpiece and bumped her head on the corner of the bookcase nearby. But still she could find no matches.

'They must be in the kitchen drawer!' she said, and off she went to look there, treading on the cat on her way, poor thing, and bumping her knee against the stool. There were no matches in the drawer, though Dame thimble felt at the back as well as at the front.

'I'll go and ask Mr Todd if he'll lend me a box,' she said at last. 'I can't *think* where mine are!'

So off she went next door to Mr Todd's. He opened the door to Dame Thimble, and when he heard that she wanted some matches, he nodded his head.

'Yes, Dame Thimble, I will lend you
some, but would you mind doing something for me in return? Would you go
along the lane to the Bee-Woman's and
ask her for a pot of her honey? She said
she would give me one today.'

'Certainly,' said Dame Thimble. So
down the lane she went till she came to
the Bee-Woman's hive-shaped cottage.
She knocked at the door and the Bee-
Woman opened it.

'Could you let me have the pot of

honey you promised Mr Todd?' asked Dame Thimble.

'Oh, yes,' said the Bee-Woman. 'But I'll have to climb to my top shelf and get it. Would you go and ask Tompkins the cat who lives next door, to lend me his new ladder? Mine is broken.'

'Very well,' said the old dame, with a sigh, and off she went next door. Tompkins the cat opened the door to her and listened to what she wanted.

'Yes,' he said. 'I will lend the Bee-Woman my ladder, but I shall want something in return. Would you go down the lane and over the hill to where Diddle the brownie lives and beg him to let me have a little of his fresh butter. I've quite run out of it today.'

'I suppose I must,' said Dame Thimble, beginning to feel very tired. 'I won't be long. Goodbye.'

She walked all the way down the lane and over the hill to Diddle the Brownie's. She told him that Tompkins the cat had sent her to borrow a little fresh butter, and Diddle promised to

146

get it from his dairy.

'Whilst I'm getting it, would you mind just popping next door to get a paper bag for it?' said Diddle. 'I haven't one.'

So Dame Thimble popped next door, and got a fine big paper bag from Twinkle the pixie, who, strangely enough, didn't want anything done in return!

Diddle put the butter into the paper bag and Dame Thimble took it, walked over the hill and up the lane, and at last came to the cottage of Tompkins the cat.

He had fetched his ladder and he gave it to Dame Thimble. She took it to the Bee-Woman, and helped her to raise it up to her top shelf. The Bee-Woman took down a small jar of honey from the shelf and handed it to Dame Thimble.

Then the old woman hurried to Mr Todd's cottage, and gave him the honey.

'Now, will you lend me some matches, Mr Todd?' she asked. 'I really must have some to light my lamp.'

'Well, it's a funny thing now, but I can't seem to find my matches,' said Mr Todd. 'They're in the bedroom somewhere. Let's go and look for them together, Dame Thimble. I'll take my kitchen candle with me.'

So they went together into the bedroom, Mr Todd carrying his candle – but just as they entered the room the draught blew out the candle! And there they both were in the darkness!

'Well, *now* we're in a fix!' cried Mr Todd. 'We shall go bumping into everything. Oh, dear, where can those matches be? We can't see to look for anything now, it's such a nuisance. We can't even light the candle till we've got some matches.'

Now at that very moment Dame Thimble put her hand in her pocket, and what was her delight to feel a box of matches there! She took them out and struck one.

'Look, I've some matches in my pocket, Mr Todd! Now we can light the candle and hunt properly.'

So they hunted with the lighted candle, but no matches could they find anywhere. Mr Todd got quite hot and bothered, and he took out his handkerchief to wipe his forehead – and out of his pocket fell – a box of matches!

'Oh, there they are!' he cried. 'They were in my pocket all the time!'

'You stupid, silly creature!' cried Dame Thimble, quite losing her temper. 'Here I've been going down on my hands and knees, poking in all the dusty corners of your bedroom and you had them in your pocket all the time! You are a big stupid, the biggest I've ever met. Fancy hunting all over the

149

# Dame Thimble and Her Matches

place for matches when they were in your pocket all the time! Why you didn't look there first I can't think! If I hadn't had my *matches* with me we couldn't even have lit your candle!'

Mr Todd wiped his forehead and looked at Dame Thimble.

'Well,' he said, 'if you had your matches in your pocket all the time, why did you come here to borrow mine?'

Dame Thimble stared at Mr Todd. Dear me, what a very peculiar thing! Here she had been scolding him for doing exactly what she had done herself! She had popped her matches safely in her pocket so that she might find them easily, and then she had hunted all over her own cottage for them. . . which was just what Mr Todd had done. And she had called him stupid and silly, when she was just as bad herself!

'Oh my, oh my!' she groaned, sinking down into a chair, 'I'm much sillier than you, Mr Todd. I've fetched honey from the Bee-Woman, a ladder from Tompkins the cat, a pat of butter from Diddle, and a paper bag from his next-door neighbour – and all because I didn't look in my pocket for my matches. I could cry, really I could!'

'No, don't do that,' said Mr Todd kindly. 'Stay to supper with me instead, and we'll have hot cocoa and new bread and honey. You'd like that. We're two foolish people, so we ought to get on very well, and understand one another nicely.'

So down they sat to hot cocoa and new bread and honey, and the very next week they got married – all because of a box of matches. Well, well, strange things do happen, don't they?

# 13

## *How John Got His Ducklings*

John lived on a farm, and he liked it very much. He loved old Dobbin the cart-horse, Bessie the donkey, and Daisy, Clover and Primrose the three brown and white cows. He loved the white sheep in the fields, and the brown hens and white ducks that wandered about everywhere.

Best of all he liked the baby animals and birds. He was always wanting some for his very, very own. But his father wouldn't let him have any.

'No, John,' he said. 'You're not old enough. You wouldn't look after them properly. You'd forget to feed them or something. Wait till you are old enough.'

'But, Daddy, I'm old enough now,' said John. 'I would feed them and water them well, Daddy, really I would. Just let me have two or three yellow chicks for my own, or some of those little yellow ducks. Do Daddy.'

But Daddy shook his head, and John knew it was no use saying any more.

So he contented himself with trying to help Daddy feed the animals, and running after Jim, the yard-man, when he went to make the pig-meal or hen food. But all the same he longed and longed to have something that was really and truly his own.

One day Jim went to cart straw for the stables. John thought he would cart straw too. He had a little wooden cart and wooden horse. He could fill the cart with straw and then pull it along by dragging the horse after him. He could put the straw in the dog's kennel.

So he piled straw into his wooden cart. The straw was away in the field

beyond the duck-pond, and it was quite a distance from the dog's kennel. When John had filled the cart he picked up the string tied to his wooden horse's neck and began to pull it – but dear me, just as he reached the hawthorn hedge not far from the pond, the horse caught its wooden stand sharply against a stone and cracked it in half.

'Oh!' said John, in dismay. 'It's broken! Poor old wooden Dobbin! I'll take you to Jim. Perhaps he can mend you for me tonight.'

He took the horse from the cart, and, leaving the cart of straw behind him, he ran off to find Jim.

'Yes, I'll mend it for you sometime, little master,' said Jim. 'But not tonight.'

He took the horse from John. By that time it was dinner-time, and John had to run indoors to wash. He forgot all about the cart he had left out in the fields.

There it stood, all by itself, full of straw. Nobody saw it, for nobody went that way. It stayed there quite forgotten until one fine morning when a big white duck squeezed herself through the hawthorn hedge and waddled over to the cart to see what it was.

When she spied the straw inside, she jumped into the cart very clumsily and sat down. What a fine place to lay an

egg! Ha, this was better than any place the other ducks had got! She laid a beautiful big greeny-grey egg there and then sat on it for a little while before she went back to the pond.

Each day the duck came to the little wooden cart that stood under the shelter of the hawthorn hedge, and laid a nice big egg there. Soon there were twelve, and the duck looked at them proudly.

She made up her mind to sit on them

and keep them warm. So every morning very early, long before anyone was up to milk the cows, the duck waddled off from the pond and sat on her eggs. She just fitted the wooden cart nicely, and she liked the straw inside because it made such a nice nest for her eggs.

John waited and waited for Jim to mend his little wooden horse - and after some weeks, Jim did at last mend it. And then John had to hunt for his wooden cart! He had quite forgotten where he had left it.

He hunted here and he hunted there. Nobody had seen it, and it was a puzzle where to look for it!

'I say, John!' called Daddy, 'You might look out for ducks' eggs whilst you're hunting for your cart. I think one of the ducks has been laying away each day, and she may have a nest somewhere.'

'I'll look hard, Daddy,' said John.

'You can have the eggs for yourself if you find them,' said Daddy.

Oooh! If only John could find them! But he knew how clever ducks were at laying eggs in places he couldn't find or couldn't get at, so he hadn't much hope of finding a nest of them.

Suddenly he remembered where he had left his wooden cart. Of course! He had been carting straw like Jim when his horse had broken. He must have left his cart somewhere out in the field where the straw was.

Off he ran - and sure enough there was his little wooden cart by the hawthorn hedge, just where he had left it all those weeks ago. Hurray!

John ran to it - and when he reached it, he stood and stared - for there was something in his cart! It was a big, fat, white duck, sitting contentedly on the

straw in his toy cart!

John looked and looked, and the duck looked back. She knew John and liked him – so she didn't mind when he slipped his hand under her and felt in the straw.

'Eggs!' said John. 'A whole nest of them! Oh, and Daddy said I might keep them if I found them! Oh, how lovely! I might have some ducklings of my own at last!'

He took hold of the shafts of the cart and gently wheeled it through the gap in the hedge to where Daddy was working near the pond.

'Daddy! Look!' called John. Daddy looked – and *how* surprised he was to see John with a cart in which a big white duck was sitting!

'She's got a whole lot of eggs!' said John. 'Can I have them, Daddy? I should think they will soon hatch into ducklings!'

'Well, well, well!' said Daddy, smiling. 'There's a find for you! Yes, you can have them, John, since you found them. But take your cart back to where you found it, or the duck won't go on sitting.'

So John took the cart back, and the duck said 'Quack,' which meant 'Thank you,' John was sure.

One day the eggs hatched into yellow ducklings, the fluffiest, prettiest little things you ever saw – twelve of them! They follow John about all day long!

Does he look after them well? Of course he does! He has never forgotten once to feed them or to give them water. Daddy says he will make a splendid farmer when he grows up.

'I shall always love ducklings best,' John says, 'because they were the first things I had for my very own. And I'll never, never give my little wooden cart away, because it was there I found the eggs!'

# 14

## *Goldie and the Toys*

Once there was a canary in a cage. The bird was as yellow as gold, so he was called Goldie. He belonged to Eric and Hilda, and they were very fond of him; they cleaned out his cage every day and gave him fresh food and water.

Now every night he used to watch the toys come alive and play with one another. He would peep out of his cage with his bright black eyes and long to get out and play with the dolls and animals. They had such good times.

'Do open my cage door and let me out!' he would beg each night. 'I want to dance with the curly-haired doll! I want to ride in that big train! I want to wind up the musical box and hear it sing. Oh, do let me out, toys!'

But they wouldn't, for they knew that he might escape out of the nursery, and then Eric and Hilda would be very sad. So they shook their heads and went on playing by themselves.

But one night, after Christmas, there was a new toy in the nursery. This was a green duck, and it liked the look of the yellow canary very much. So when the little bird began to call out to the toys to let it out of its cage, the duck spoke up.

'Why don't we let the canary out to have a bit of fun with us? After all, the poor thing is stuck in its cage all day long and never gets a chance to play a game? I'd like to be friends with it. I'm a bird too, and I should like a good long chat with another bird.'

'Yes, yes!' cried the canary eagerly. 'Let me out, duck! I am so lonely up here! I should love a chat with a beautiful bird like you!'

'The windows and the door are shut,' said the big doll. 'I don't see that it will do any harm. The canary couldn't

escape out of the room if it wanted to!'

'I don't want to escape!' cried the canary. 'I just want to have a game. I will go back to my cage when everything is over.'

'Very well,' said the biggest doll. 'You shall come out and join us this evening – but remember, if you don't behave properly, we'll never let you out again!'

The canary promised to be good, and the toy clown threw a rope up to the cage, and then climbed right up it. He opened the door and out flew Goldie, simply delighted to stretch his wings and have a fly round.

You should have seen how Goldie enjoyed himself. The toys set the musical box going and when the tune was tinkled out the canary took hold of the curly-haired doll with his wing and off they danced together over the nursery floor. The canary really danced very well indeed, for he was so light on his feet.

After they had had a good dance, the clockwork train offered to take the toys for a ride. Of course, the canary wanted to drive, and, my goodness me, he drove so fast that the train couldn't see where it was going, and bumped into a chair leg. Out fell all the toys in a heap, and they were not very pleased with the canary. He didn't get bumped at all because as soon as he saw the engine was going to run into the chair leg he simply spread his wings and flew safely into the air!

Then the toys played hide-and-seek, and the canary liked that very much because he could fly up to the top of the curtains, or on to the clock, and no toy thought of looking there for him, so he was the only one that was never caught. He *did* enjoy himself.

At last cock-crow came, when all the toys had to go back to the toy-cupboard and sleep.

'It's time to go back to your cage, Goldie,' said the big doll; 'You've had a

lovely time, haven't you? Just fly back
to your cage now, there's a good bird,
and let the clockwork clown shut your
door.'

'Not I!' said Goldie cheekily. 'I'm not
going back to my cage for hours and
HOURS and HOURS. No, I'm going to
stay in the nursery and fly about as
long as I like!'

'But you promised!' cried the toys.

'I don't care!' said the naughty
canary.

168

'How dreadful to break a promise!' said the green duck, who was feeling hurt because the canary had hardly spoken a word to him. 'I wonder you're not ashamed of yourself. Go back to your cage at once.'

But the canary simply wouldn't. He just flew away as soon as any toy came near him. It was most annoying.

'We shall have to do *something*!' said the big doll in despair. 'If we leave him loose like this he will fly out of the door in the morning when the housemaid opens it, and then the cat will get him! What *can* we do?'

They all whispered together, and then at last the clockwork clown had an idea.

'Let's spread the table in the dolls' house, and say we're going to have supper there,' he said. 'The canary will want to join us, of course – and we'll get him in. Then we'll all go out and slam the door. He will have to stay in the dolls' house till morning then.'

'Splendid idea!' cried all the toys.

They ran to the dolls' house, and began to lay the cloth. They set out the tiny cups, saucers and plates, and then the big doll fetched some sweets from the toy sweet-shop.

'What are you doing?' cried the canary from his perch on a candlestick.

'We're going to have supper,' said the clockwork clown.

'Well, I'm coming too,' said the canary. Down he flew and hopped in at the front door of the dolls' house. The curly-haired doll saw that all the windows were tightly shut, and the clockwork clown stuffed up the chimney with paper so that Goldie couldn't escape that way.

The canary sat down on a chair, and the big doll gave him a sweet on his plate. He put it into his beak, and didn't notice that one by one all the toys were creeping out of the house. At last he was quite alone.

Slam! The canary jumped up in fright. The door of the dolls' house was tight shut. He was caught.

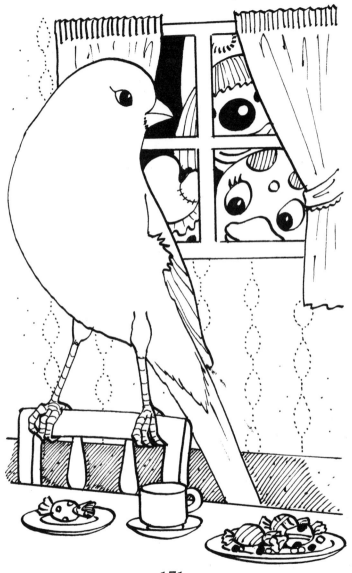

'Let me out, let me out!' he yelled.

'No,' said the toys. 'You just stay there!'

'Let me go back to my cage,' said the canary.

'No,' said the big doll at once. 'As soon as we open the door you would fly away again!'

'I promise I would go back to my cage,' said Goldie, pecking at the front door with his beak.

'We don't trust you,' said the clown. 'You broke your promise before, so we are sure you would break it again.'

Then the toys went to the toy cupboard and fell asleep. The canary hopped on to the table in the dolls' house and went to sleep too.

In the morning Eric and Hilda came into the nursery – and the first thing they saw was the open door of the canary's cage. How upset they were!

'Goldie's gone, Goldie's gone!' they cried. 'Oh, where can he be?'

Goldie heard his name and he hopped about excitedly in the dolls' house, trilling loudly.

'Listen!' said Eric, astonished. 'Can you hear Goldie trilling? Where is he?'

'It sounds as if he were in the dolls' house!' said Hilda, astonished. They knelt down and peeped through the window – and there they saw Goldie, hopping about inside the little house.

'There he is!' said Eric. 'But however did he get there? What a funny thing! He can't have got in there and shut the door himself!'

The children opened the door and Eric slipped in his hand and took hold of Goldie very gently – and in two seconds the little canary was safely in his cage once more, singing very loudly indeed.

'I'm sure our big doll is smiling,' said Hilda, suddenly. 'I wonder why!'

'Perhaps she could tell us how Goldie got into the dolls' house!' said Eric.

She certainly could, couldn't she? You may be quite sure that the toys *never* let Goldie out of his cage again. He really was much too naughty to be trusted!

173

# 15

## *Muzzling the Cat*

Once upon a time there lived a big grey cat with orange eyes. He was called Smoky because his fur was the colour of grey smoke. He used to lie on the sunny wall and watch the birds flying about in the trees.

The birds hated Smoky because he was so clever at catching them. He caught their young ones too, and that made them very miserable.

'Let's have a meeting about Smoky,' said the thrushes and blackbirds. 'Perhaps we can think of some way of stopping his dreadful deeds.'

So they called a meeting. The robin came, full of woe because one of his youngsters had been caught by Smoky the day before. The wren came, cocking

up his perky little tail. The chaffinch came with his pretty salmon-pink breast, and the starling, flashing blue and green in the sunshine. The sparrow was there too, cheeky as usual, as talkative as the starling.

'Friends,' said the big blackbird, opening his beautiful orange beak, 'we have met here today to talk about that horrid cat, Smoky.'

At once there was a great deal of

twittering and chattering.

'Silence,' said the speckled thrush, lifting up one of his feet. Everyone was quiet.

'Smoky catches us and our young ones in a very cruel way,' went on the blackbird. 'We must stop him. How shall we do this? Has anyone any good ideas?'

'Let's all fly round and peck him hard,' said the robin, fiercely.

'Well - that would only make him angrier still the next day,' said the blackbird. 'He would probably kill us all!'

'Let's upset his dish of milk each morning!' cried the wren.

'That's no good!' said the blackbird. 'He would be so hungry that he would catch us all the more!'

There was silence for a moment - and then the sparrow and the starling both spoke at once. 'Let's - let's - let's -' Then they stopped and glared at one another. They opened their beaks once more. 'Let's. . . let's. . .'

The starling pecked the sparrow. 'Will you be quiet and let *me* speak?' he shouted.

The sparrow pecked at the starling. 'You let *me* speak!' he answered back sharply.

'Order, order!' said the thrush sharply. 'No quarrelling here!'

'My idea is very good,' said the

starling hurriedly. 'Why not MUZZLE the cat?'

'That was my idea, too!' cried the sparrow in a rage. 'I was going to say EXACTLY the same thing!'

'You see,' said the starling, taking no notice of the sparrow, 'if the cat wears a muzzle, it cannot eat us! There is an old dog's muzzle hanging in the garden shed. We could get that and muzzle the cat well with it.'

'A splendid idea,' said the blackbird. 'Yes, the cat shall be muzzled.'

'I thought of it first!' chirruped the sparrow, angrily, trying to peck a feather from the starling's wing.

'You're a story-teller!' squawked the starling. 'It was *my* idea!'

'Who is going to do the muzzling?' asked the thrush.

Nobody answered. Nobody wanted *that* little piece of work.

'Come, come,' said the blackbird, '*somebody* must do it.'

'Well, I think it ought to be the one who thought of the idea first,' said the thrush firmly.

The starling nearly fell off the tree with fright. The sparrow hid his head under his wing, hoping that nobody would notice he was still there.

'Er. . .er. . .' said the starling, at last. 'Well. . . as the sparrow kept saying just now – it was really *his* idea, not mine. I ought not to have spoken.'

The sparrow took his head from beneath his wing in a temper.

'Ho!' he said, 'you say it was *my* idea, now you think you've got to muzzle the cat yourself! Well. . . you can *have* the idea! I don't want it! You said it was yours, and so it is!'

'No quarrelling here!' said the black-bird. '*Both* of you shall do the muzzling together! Sparrow, go and fetch the muzzle from the garden shed.'

Off flew the sparrow, and came back with the little wire muzzle in his beak. His smart little mind had thought of an idea to trick the starling.

'Come on, starling!' he cried. 'It's no use putting it off. It's got to be done.

I'm not a coward, if you are!'

The starling shivered with fright.

'Look,' said the sparrow, 'I've got the muzzle ready – but I can't muzzle the cat by myself, starling. You must go and hold him still whilst I put it on. Come on!' The starling gave a great splutter of fright. Hold that cat still! Oooooh! The very thought made the starling feel quite faint.

'Do hurry up!' chirruped the sparrow. 'Smoky is lying on the wall. Just fly

down and hold him tightly by the neck.
Then, as soon as he is quite still I will
slip the muzzle over his mouth.'

'Yes, hurry and help the sparrow!'
cried all the other birds to the frightened
starling.

But he didn't dare to. He spread his
wings and flew squawking and splut-
tering away, leaving the sparrow and
the muzzle behind him.

'Coward! Coward!' cried all the birds.

The sparrow was delighted. 'Come
along, somebody!' he cried. 'I don't
mind who holds the cat still for me.
Will *you,* blackbird?'

'I've got to go back to see my wife,'
said the blackbird, in a hurry, and he
flew off. And before very long the
sparrow was left quite alone, chuckling
and chirruping to himself in delight.

Then he heard a voice below him
that made him tremble with fear.

'Ho, little sparrow, I heard all that
has been said,' said Smoky the cat,
with a laugh. 'How cowardly all the
birds are except you, aren't they? Well,

you shall show them how brave you are! I promise to keep quite still, and you shall try to muzzle me. So come down and do what you want to!'

But alas! The sparrow had fled! The muzzle had dropped down to the ground, and Smoky yawned widely showing his sharp white teeth.

'A fuss about nothing!' he said. 'They are all as cowardly as each other. I shall go and get my bread and milk.'

Have you ever heard the starlings talking loudly to one another, or the sparrows twittering in a crowd among the trees? You'll know what they are talking about now. . . how the cat was NEARLY muzzled – but not quite!

# 16

## *The Real Live Fairy Doll*

Gwen and Peter were very much excited because they were going to have a big Christmas tree that Christmas. What fun!

'Will it have a fairy doll at the top, Mummy?' asked Gwen. 'I do hope it will.'

'You shall have a fairy doll at the very top!' said Mummy, 'and lots of toys and candles all over the tree.'

That night Daddy and Mummy went

out to buy the tree and all the things to hang on it. They bought the prettiest fairy doll you ever saw, with wings of silver, and a dress that shone and glittered. She was to go at the top of the tree.

All the toys were hung on the tree, and the candles were slipped into their stands and clipped on to the branches. The doll was fastened to the very tip, and how grand she looked, shining there. Mummy and Daddy were very pleased.

The toys in the nursery sat and looked at the tree in delight, when Mummy and Daddy had gone downstairs. They thought they had never in all their life seen such a pretty thing. As for the fairy doll, they thought she was the loveliest toy in the world.

Then a most dreadful thing happened. What do you think? The poor fairy doll was not fastened tightly enough to the tree, and suddenly she felt herself falling!

'Help! Help!' she squealed.

But nobody could help her. She fell – she slid between the branches of the Christmas tree and landed with a

bump on the floor. All the toys rushed to pick her up.

But oh, dear me, she had broken both her nice little legs! What a dreadful thing!

'Whatever shall we do?' said the teddy bear. 'Is there time for her to be mended before the children have the tree tomorrow night?'

'Let's go and ask the elf who lives under the nursery window,' said the giraffe. 'She knows a lot. Perhaps she could mend the fairy doll.'

So they called her in. She came dancing into the nursery and looked at the poor broken doll crying on the floor.

'I will take her to the Mend-Up Gnome,' she said. 'He will soon mend her nicely. She will be quite all right in twenty-four hours' time.'

'Twenty-four hours!' cried the toys. 'Goodness, won't the children be disappointed. They *did* so want a fairy doll to stand at the top of their Christmas tree tomorrow night!'

Everyone stood looking very gloomy

- and then the giraffe spoke up. He turned to the elf and said: 'I say! Would *you* take the fairy doll's place do you think? You have silvery wings like hers and your dress is all shiny and glittering too. You would have a fine time at the top of the tree and you would see everything that was going on.'

'Well,' said the elf, thoughtfully, 'well - let me see. Yes - I think I could do that for you. I love boys and girls and it would be fun to see them all dancing round the tree and having their presents. I'll just take this doll to old Mend-Up, and then I'll come back and fly up to the top of the tree!'

You should have seen how lovely she looked up there! The toys looked and looked and looked at her - and when the party began the next day, how all the children stared to see such a beautiful fairy doll at the top of the tree!

She had a lovely time. She watched the children dancing - and do you

know what she did when the grown-ups had gone out of the room to have some supper, and had left the children by themselves? She flew down from the tree, took hands with them and danced all round the tree, singing a little magic song in a high, silvery voice.

The children were surprised and pleased.

'I say! That's a wonderful fairy doll of yours!' said one little girl to Gwen. 'My doll talks and walks, but I've never seen one that could dance and sing!'

'It's a real, live fairy; that's what it is,' said another little girl. 'It's not a doll at all!'

Just then the elf heard the grown-ups coming and she flew straight back to the top of the tree.

'Mummy!' cried Gwen. 'Do you know, the fairy doll flew down from the tree and danced and sang with us!'

'Nonsense!' said Mummy, and nobody would believe that what the children said was true.

'Well,' said Gwen to Peter, 'when

Mummy takes the fairy doll down from the tree tomorrow, she will find it is a real live fairy – and won't she be surprised?'

But the little fairy doll came back from Mend-Up the Gnome's that night, both her legs beautifully mended, and the toys helped her to climb up to the top of the tree. The elf flew down and said goodbye to the toys.

'I *have* enjoyed myself!' she said. 'And wasn't it fun when I flew down

and danced with the children. I nearly laughed out loud to see their surprised faces!'

The next day the children begged their mother to take down the fairy doll from the tree. They felt sure it was a *real* fairy, and not a doll. But when they saw her, what a disappointment!

'It's a doll after all!' said Gwen. 'I wonder how it was she turned into a live fairy last night.'

'Don't be silly,' said Mummy, laughing. 'I don't know why you keep telling that foolish story, Gwen. No fairy doll could come down from the tree and dance and sing.'

'Well, it *must* have been a fairy then,' said Peter. 'So that settles it!'

He was quite right, wasn't he?